Dear Reader,

Do *you* have a secret fantasy? Everybody does. Maybe it's to be rich and famous and beautiful. Or to start a no-strings affair with a sexy mysterious stranger. Or to have a sizzling second chance with a former sweetheart.... You'll find these dreams—and much more—in Temptation's exciting new yearlong promotion, Secret Fantasies.

Debra Carroll has taken the "trapped in the same house" story line and added gothic and fantasy twists. A gorgeous, noble hero and a heroine badly burned by love light sparks off each other hot enough to sizzle the pages! The result is a romantic delight that will make this book a "keeper" on your shelves.

In the coming months, look for Secret Fantasies books by Lisa Harris, Glenda Sanders and JoAnn Ross. Please write and let us know how you enjoy the "fantasy."

Happy Reading!

The Editors

c/o Harlequin Temptation
225 Duncan Mill Road
Don Mills, Ontario
M3B 3K9
Canada

Dear Reader,

What is one of the most powerful secret fantasies? Is it falling in love with, say, Mel Gibson, or having Mel fall madly, deeply, head-over-heels in love with you? And more than that, to have the power of bringing him to his knees when you say no. (Pretend you're strong enough to "just say no." Pretend *harder*.)

Well, it isn't Emma Jordan's fantasy. She doesn't believe in anything anymore, especially love. But Sam Cooper is not the man to leave her alone with her secrets, especially when he finds himself madly, deeply, head-over-heels in love with her. Obsessed.

And Emma, too, is obsessed, even horrified, by the power of her desire for him. This obsession forces them into exploring the dark, dangerous side of fantasy and love.

Working on this book, with these characters, has been so much fun. Of course, researching the background was arduous—long solitary rambles through the woods, watching sunsets over the lake. You get the picture, it was hell. We edited this book on a porch, amid dogs, construction and a constant stream of teenagers, but the view was wonderful—not the least bit scary. Although, as Sam discovers, there are places where the woods are dark and the trail is lonely, and he finds himself playing the part usually reserved for the Gothic heroine.

As new authors with Temptation, we're very excited about our first book, *Obsession*. This is a very special story for us, a way to explore the boundless power of love—the power to make us infinitely vulnerable and the power to heal the deepest wounds.

We hope you enjoy *Obsession*.

Best wishes,

Debra Carroll

"Emma," Sam said softly. "This isn't working."

She could feel the heat of his body so close to her, his warm breath stirring the tendrils of hair curling around her cheek. "I can't sleep at night for dreaming of you. And during the day, just being near you...hurts." Longing grated in his low husky voice.

"No, Sam," she cried in anguish. "Stay away from me."

"I can't. I need to touch you." His hands were shaking as they closed on her upper arms.

She shut her eyes in the agony of wanting, frantically fighting the need for fulfillment throbbing deep inside. Giving in would be her downfall.

His hot mouth grazed her jaw and she had to will herself not to turn in his arms. But now his muscled length was pressed against her back and she felt herself weakening. She tried again. "You said we could fight this."

"We should." He turned her around and she stared spellbound into his glittering eyes. "But it's so much easier to just give in," he whispered as his mouth came down on hers.

Debra Carroll is really two people: Carol Bruce-Thomas and Debra McCarthy-Anderson. Friends forever, five years ago the pair decided they wanted to do something new and interesting with their lives. Rather like Mickey Rooney to Judy Garland, one said to the other, "I know, let's write a romance!" They set a five-year goal to sell to Harlequin. Along the way, they sold two romance novels under the name of Rachel Vincer to Meteor Books. And then, with eight days to spare in the five-year deadline, Harlequin phoned and offered them a contract for *Obsession*. The Temptation editors are very excited by this extremely talented writing duo and pleased that the book fit so well into our Secret Fantasies miniseries. Look for the next book by Debra Carroll at Christmas!

OBSESSION
DEBRA CARROLL

Harlequin Books

TORONTO • NEW YORK • LONDON
AMSTERDAM • PARIS • SYDNEY • HAMBURG
STOCKHOLM • ATHENS • TOKYO • MILAN
MADRID • WARSAW • BUDAPEST • AUCKLAND

To Jenny and Martin:

Thanks for the use of your porch and all the wonderful country rambles around Fenelon Falls

ISBN 0-373-25626-4

OBSESSION

This edition published by arrangement with Harlequin Enterprises B.V.

® and TM are trademarks of the publisher. Trademarks indicated with ® are registered in the United States Patent and Trademark Office, the Canadian Trade Marks Office and in other countries.

Printed in U.S.A.

1

SAM GRASPED the cool black-metal tracery of the imposing wrought-iron gates and rattled, hard. Everything he had, everything he'd worked for was riding on this project, and Emma Jordan was jerking him around out of sheer perverse pleasure.

Damn. He gritted his teeth in frustration and gave one more futile push at the unyielding metal. Locked up tighter than that old witch's heart.

No buzzer, no intercom on either of the fieldstone gate-posts, just a tall iron fence that summed up everything he'd been butting his head against for the last three months. He took a couple of deep breaths and forced himself to relax, to let go of the tension making a knot of the muscles in his neck and shoulders.

Suddenly the buzz-saw whine of cicadas filled the sultry evening air and then, just as abruptly, stopped. All at once he became aware of the eerie quiet. Looking down the lonely winding road that disappeared into the trees on the other side of the gate, a cold chill went creeping down his back, despite the heat of the evening that pressed down like a hot, stifling blanket. Beads of sweat prickled on his upper lip.

Almost with longing, he cast a glance back over his shoulder, beyond the rented four-by-four to the country road that had brought him here. The town of Fenelon Falls was only a mile or so away. It wasn't too late to turn around and go back to safety.

Did he say *safety*? He gave a wry chuckle, but standing there, dwarfed by the massive iron gates, he knew it was an uneasy attempt to shake off that creepy feeling that had snuck in under his frustration, even as he cursed himself for being a fool.

On the other hand, who could blame him? The woman could hardly be normal. The perverse erotic horror that filled her book didn't come from imagination alone. You couldn't sell him on that. Just like Mary Shelley was no typical schoolgirl when she wrote *Frankenstein.* If Emma Jordan turned out to be some sweet, rosy-cheeked little grand-mother, he'd eat his favorite Dodgers cap.

He'd spent the flight from L.A. and the two-hour drive from Toronto replaying every nuance of the screenplay ne-gotiations, trying to get a handle on the infuriating woman.

At best she must be some kind of crackpot, not quite in touch with the real world. Then he could blame her shark of an agent for giving him the gears. Petra Moscovia knew damn well that he wanted *Belial* so bad he'd do almost anything to get it.

But that didn't absolve Emma Jordan of arrogance. All that phony crap about the integrity of her work being worth more than money, forcing him to jack up the price yet again.

It still made him clench his teeth in frustration, remem-bering the way she'd backed him into a corner until he had no choice but to agree to spend six weeks with her, writing the screenplay, *and* give her final approval. All without even the courtesy of speaking to him directly.

He rested his cheek against the cool metal tracery of the gate. It felt good on his hot, sweaty face. He closed his eyes and took a deep breath. The air smelled lush and fragrant as the quiet descended around him. He felt so tired.

Over the past few months sleep had been a stranger to him and loneliness a constant companion. His eyes snapped open. No. He didn't want to start thinking in that direction.

Instead he took a closer look at the gate, an impressive, even intimidating structure rearing high above his head. He hadn't noticed before, but now he saw, worked into the tracery, twin gargoyles gazing down at him.

Anyone who lived behind gates this high had a lot to protect or, more likely, a lot to hide. So what was Emma Jordan hiding?

The old eccentric wouldn't stir from her lair in the Kawartha Lakes, even to promote a runaway bestselling novel, wouldn't even allow her photo on the book jacket, and then reaped a mountain of publicity from the tactic.

One corner of his mouth lifted in a humorless quirk. Why not? It worked for Garbo. *I vant to be alone.*

But it was more than just a wish for privacy. No, there had to be something very bizarre about a woman whose work showed such an intimate acquaintance with evil.

"State your business."

The menacing, guttural rasp made him spin around, and the breath left his body in a sharp rush. The hulking figure of a man loomed in the twilight. A man built on a monumental scale, towering head and shoulders above Sam. With a massive, barrel-chested body, powerful arms and ham-size fists that looked like they could wrap right around his neck and snap it as easily as plucking a daisy.

My God. Had his thoughts of Mary Shelley conjured up her monster?

All at once he remembered to breathe. "I'm ..." He swallowed in annoyance at his cracking voice. "I'm Sam Cooper."

That face! Above the battered nose, many times broken, sunken eyes gleamed from under a protruding brow. And most shocking of all, a mass of rough, shining scar tissue pulled up one corner of his mouth into a permanent sneer.

"Prove it."

For a moment Sam could only gawk. No one had asked him to do that for a very long time. His face was generally proof enough.

"My ID is in the car." Sam edged toward the Jeep Cherokee, half expecting the monster to stop him. But the man only stood there waiting, eyeing him, still without a hint of recognition.

Never taking his eyes from the watchful giant, he reached into the glove compartment with hands that were suddenly clumsy. He extracted his driver's license and handed it over, while keeping a wary distance.

No wonder his heart was still pounding. Having a creature like this materialize in these eerie surroundings, while his head was filled with thoughts of the sinister Emma Jordan, was enough to frighten anyone.

The man took the license and carefully examined it. He really looked like something from a horror movie. Sam couldn't take his eyes off the hideous scars. My God, hadn't the guy heard of plastic surgery?

Then the deep-set eyes shifted upward, met Sam's stare and filled with contempt as they looked him slowly up and down. It was hard to meet the other man's gaze. He felt stupid and ashamed of himself.

After a lengthy, silent inspection the giant finally nodded and handed back his credentials. "Drive on."

Whatever conclusions he had drawn, the gatekeeper was clearly unimpressed as he turned to walk away, heading for a small white house tucked under the trees so discreetly that Sam only noticed it now.

Even in the twilight he could see the bright splashes of color in the flower-filled boxes at every pristine lace-curtained window. The keeper of the gate lived in this fairy-tale cottage? He rubbed his eyes and looked again. Maybe he was still on the plane, dreaming.

But no. With a low electric hum the big gates began to open.

"Hell," he muttered as he backed away. "This is getting weirder and weirder." What was he getting himself into?

Back in the lifesaving coolness of the air-conditioned car, he let out a deep breath. He'd better snap out of it. Stop letting his imagination give him the creeps.

He'd mortgaged his soul for this shot at getting off the mindless treadmill of action movies. While he'd be forever grateful for the financial rewards and recognition they had brought him, now he needed more. A real challenge. A chance to stretch his creative muscles.

And, since no one else believed in him enough to give him a chance, he'd make his own chances.

He drove through the gate, into the gloom cast by the heavy canopy of white pines and maples. Winding through the trees, he rounded a turn and suddenly found himself back in the fading light of a fuchsia sky as the road crossed a narrow causeway. The still, gray waters of the lake spread out on either side.

His dark mood lifted a little. Jays flashed blue among the pines, water lilies floated serenely on the sheltered side of the peninsula. Whatever Emma Jordan's neuroses, he couldn't blame her for wanting to live amid all this natural beauty.

Back under the trees again, he could see a gleam of white ahead and finally pulled up where the gravel widened out in front of a rambling Victorian clapboard house commanding the tip of the point. Not the gothic horror he half expected, but a distinctive, gracious old home, with a wraparound veranda trimmed with scrolled white gingerbread and hanging flower baskets.

He parked by a two-door garage at the side of the house, shelving his morbid fantasies as he got out of the car and walked briskly up the steps to the deep wooden porch. His eyes felt gritty with fatigue and the muscles in his legs ached from hours of confinement. It had been a long day, a long drive, and he could use a long sleep.

Any moment now he would finally come face-to-face with Emma Jordan. It was time to unload the emotional baggage, bury all the self-doubt and frustration she had caused him. Now was his chance to change her opinion. Working with her wouldn't be easy, but he'd do his damnedest to keep things running smoothly. The important thing was coming up with a good script. He had a lot to prove, not only to the studio, but to himself.

He opened the screen door and gave three loud raps on the brass knocker. While he waited he turned to look around him at the grounds, dotted with massive oaks and maples, sloping down to the still lake. It was so quiet.

And the house was equally still. He turned back to peer through the lace-covered glass panel in the front door, then knocked again.

There were no lights on, no sign of life at all. The quiet was truly unnatural. There were no birds singing. No sound of lapping water. No rustling of leaves. As if the world were holding its breath in the waiting twilight. That spooky feeling started creeping up on him again and it took conscious effort to quell it. Instead he knocked, much louder, in defiance of the quiet. The sound echoed in the dead air around him.

He sighed, impatient with his fantasies. Let's face it, she wasn't home. He'd knocked loud enough to wake the dead. He let the screen door go in disgust and walked over to lean on the porch rail, clenching his jaw in frustration.

"Damn you! Where are you?"

He'd crossed a continent at the demand of Emma Jordan and now her majesty wasn't even here! He had every right to feel hot, tired and pissed-off. Was this just another demonstration that she had all the power?

He quelled the impulse to take it out on the porch railing and turned back to look at the silent house, the closed door mocking him. A humorless smile curved his mouth.

"Maybe you *are* home, huh? Maybe you're just waiting for the sun to go down." He gave an impatient snort, "You dumb jerk," and ran a hand through his short hair, damp and spiky with sweat. "Not only does she have you twisted into knots, she's got you talking to yourself, too."

He took a deep breath and tried to calm down. There was no point in getting all worked up; it was too hot for that. It was an effort just to pull the sticky air into his lungs. The oppressive humidity weighed down like a thick wet blanket. This felt more like the steamy Mississippi Delta than anything he'd ever experienced in Ontario.

There was nothing for it but to wait until she got back, unless he wanted to return to the gate and cross-examine Frankenstein.

On second thought, he'd wait.

He slowly walked down the porch stairs to the grass. Past nine and the sky was still light, but it had darkened to a deep clear blue above his head. He'd forgotten this long northern twilight.

Suddenly a sweetly mournful call pierced the silence. From somewhere off across the lake echoed the clear, beautiful song of the loon. The haunting sound raised goose bumps on his flesh as he followed it down toward the water, picking his way carefully over the protruding roots of the massive trees and around the mossy boulders.

Robyn would have loved it here. She wouldn't have seen anything sinister in this setting. She would have told him to let the peace seep in, let it cleanse all the stress.

He stopped at the base of a giant willow that overhung the water. One massive limb jutted out sideways, creating a comfortable seat. He sat down, leaning his back against the trunk, and looked around. Farther along, across a strip of sandy beach, perched a chalet-style boathouse with a colorful garden planted around it. His gaze swept across the timeless landscape, once again struck by the beauty of these lakes, gouged by glaciers from the ancient bedrock of the Canadian Shield.

The water was glassy calm and out in the middle of the lake a lone canoe made a dark silhouette against the last red glow in the western sky. He took a deep breath of the sweet, pine-scented air and slowly exhaled, feeling calmer already. No wonder Emma Jordan didn't want to leave this haven.

But that didn't explain the mystery surrounding her, the gatekeeper guaranteed to frighten, the seclusion, her refusal to even speak to him on the phone. Who could blame him for all his dark imaginings? But he wouldn't allow his imagination or anything else to get in the way of what he'd come here to do.

Ever since Robyn died a year ago, he'd been a changed man. All those things that had once given him pleasure and satisfaction with his job—being number one at the box office, the highest-paid male star in Hollywood—meant nothing now.

Not that it had ever been about money. Beyond helping out the people he cared for and making a comfortable living, the money didn't mean that much.

Now, after losing the woman he loved at the age of thirty-six, the woman he'd planned to spend the rest of his life with, he knew that no material wealth could fill that empty, aching space inside.

He needed something else. Not another relationship—it was much too soon for that—but a challenge in his life. And the night he read Emma Jordan's book, he knew he'd found it.

That story had grabbed him and wouldn't let go. Maybe it was the work of destiny, the February blizzard that had closed down J. F. Kennedy Airport, marooning him in Josh's Manhattan apartment, driving him to idly pick up the reviewer's galleys of *Belial* off his friend's coffee table.

He'd read it in one sitting, spellbound. There and then, he had realized that *this* was the vehicle he'd been searching for, without even knowing it. Something as far as possible from the simplistic shoot-'em-ups and uncomplicated characters he had tackled so far. Josh's review hit it on the button. It really was "a compelling, seductive, dark fantasy, laced with a bitter awareness of the world's evil."

He knew he could make that magic work on the screen, felt it in his guts. The result would be unique, unlike anything out there. The studio would back him to the skies—if he wanted to direct as well as star in the next film in his phenomenally successful *Demolition* series. But they wouldn't put a penny into a risky property like *Belial*.

Robyn would have believed. She would have been pushing him to challenge himself, to take the risks.

Well, he was doing it. Putting practically everything he had into the project. And he still needed to find more backing. But without a dynamite script, no one else would risk a dime on him.

He snapped off one of the long, narrow willow fronds hanging over his head. The trouble was that self-doubt was starting to get to him. There were moments when he was almost crippled by the fear that he really was biting off more than he could chew.

Even though he told himself that they were wrong, that he could do it, now that Robyn was gone, he only had himself to depend on.

In the early days he'd been brash and thick-skinned, too driven to give a damn about anyone else's opinion. But back then no one expected anything of him, he had nothing to prove. Now, too many careers and too much money was riding on him.

The studio's reluctance he could understand, but to have Emma Jordan making the same kind of assumptions, without knowing anything about his capabilities . . .

He stood, restless again as the familiar feeling of frustration gripped him. He began walking back toward the house via the lagoon side of the point where water lilies glowed pale and creamy against the dark water, trying to rid himself of the insidious feeling. It was not productive.

As for Emma Jordan, she could be any kind of weirdo she wanted to be, high priestess of a flesh-eating cult for all he cared. She had written a brilliant book, and he could turn it into a brilliant screenplay, no matter what anybody said to the contrary.

The spicy fragrance of wildflowers and damp earth filled his nostrils as his feet sank into the mossy ground beneath the trees. It was darker now and more difficult to see where he was walking. The heat weighed down, holding everything still. Beneath the cotton shirt he could feel his skin prickling with the humidity.

He paused for a moment and turned to look at the lake. The canoe had vanished. Not a breath of wind ruffled the smooth water reflecting the last delicate tints of the western sky.

Suddenly a small dark shape swooped down silently from above. Instinctively he threw up his hands to protect his head, ducked and swerved out of the way. To his horror, one foot encountered only thin air.

He fell, reaching out in vain to save himself, realizing at that instant what the creature had been—a bat!

He landed hard, spread-eagled on his back, and for what seemed like long, agonizing minutes he couldn't breathe, conscious only of the viselike pain gripping his chest and back, as if someone had driven a stake through his rib cage.

Winded. That was all. He was only winded. It had happened to him often enough on the set.

Slowly, he dragged a little air into his seared lungs and stared up at the darkening sky, framed in black. A perfect rectangle. The shape of a freshly-dug grave.

You moron.

Gingerly he tried to move his arms and legs. For a brief eternity they didn't seem to be responding, then he realized he was embedded in a thick layer of gooey, slimy mud.

It had probably saved him from breaking his neck. He'd have been grateful, if he weren't so mad. This was the crowning indignity. He was beginning to wish he'd never heard the name Emma Jordan.

He slowly sat up. The blackness whirled a little, then the brief dizziness quickly receded, along with the fading pain in his lungs. Thanking God that he wasn't badly hurt, Sam scrambled to his feet, which wasn't easy in the slippery, unstable mud.

Even in daytime it would be dark in this deep hole, under the canopy of trees, but in the fast-fading light it was pitch-black. He didn't want to think about what could be sharing this pit with him. Things like snakes, or the massive wolf spiders he'd read about.

His clothes had been damp from sweat to begin with, but the summer heat didn't reach below ground and now they clung to him, dank and chilly. *The cold of the grave.*

God, he was a jerk. But a shudder went through him nevertheless. He'd seen too many movies and spent too much time recently thinking about the unsettling world of *Belial*. Rational or not, however, the thought gave him the creeps.

The top of the hole was a good three, maybe four feet above his head. He reached out and felt rough wood under his palms. He made several abortive attempts to get out, but three of the sides were shored up with vertical wooden planks and there was no way he could climb them, even if his sneakers weren't caked with slimy clay mud. The fourth side was a wall of solid concrete, and equally unscalable.

The discovery made a sick knot in the pit of his stomach. He was trapped. Trapped in this damn hole.

The sickness turned quickly to burning rage, starting in his gut and spreading throughout every inch of his body. *That bitch!*

After everything he'd been through, now he was going to have to spend the night in a pit. He punched the wooden planking and then doubled over, clutching his mangled fist in his other hand. Gritting his teeth, he waited for the burning pain to subside, fighting back the nausea and the stinging tears. Then he turned and kicked at the other side, impotent fury boiling in his veins.

Just let him get a hold of Emma Jordan. If he had to die in this hole, just let him live long enough to strangle her with his bare hands!

EMMA HAULED the battered red canoe up onto the grass, pulled off her life jacket and tossed it under the gunwale, before flipping the canoe over with practiced ease.

Out on the lake there'd been at least the hint of a breeze, but now the heat and humidity made the black T-shirt and denim cutoffs cling uncomfortably to her sweaty skin. She wanted a long, cold drink and a cool shower, in that order.

She hadn't meant to be out this late, but the loon was back on the lake. She'd tried to forget her anxieties and find solace in following its playful antics, watching it dive headfirst beneath the glassy water and then pop up again at a different spot, repeating the maneuver every time she got close.

It was the loon and writer's block keeping her out there so long, slowly paddling, not her lingering unease about Sam Cooper. Only twenty-four hours until her private world would be invaded by the man who had badgered her until he finally got what he wanted.

If her object had only been money, she wouldn't have cared that he wanted to turn her book into a movie. But it was unthinkable that Belial might be made into just another macho action-adventure hero, like all the roles Sam Cooper was famous for.

Belial was a piece of *her*, committed to paper, wrenched out of her during the darkest five weeks of her life.

If it had been Zeffirelli or Scorsese, she'd still have had her doubts, but *Sam Cooper?*

But that wasn't the worst of it. It was the thought of a stranger invading her sanctuary, the blissful solitude where she had finally found peace after her life had been shattered two years ago. Coping with this intruder would be difficult, even frightening, she finally admitted to herself.

She took a deep fortifying breath of the sweet evening air. This was a commitment. She had to stop being a coward and remember that she'd weathered much worse.

On the western horizon a thin line of crimson cloud was the only remnant left of the sunset. Above her head the sky was dotted with the first stars. It was quite dark under the trees as she headed toward the house.

"Is someone there?" Out of the darkness a disembodied voice issued from the ground almost beneath her feet. A male voice, deep and resonant. Like a voice from hell.

The pit! Her foot caught on something, she pitched violently forward and at that precise moment vividly remembered telling the workmen that they didn't need to fence off the excavation. There was no danger of anyone falling in.

Then *she* was falling, her scream precipitously cut off by her impact on a solid figure that grunted as they collapsed in a tangled heap.

For a moment she didn't move in the pitch-dark, suddenly aware of the warm, hard male body beneath her, pressed intimately against her from head to toe. Her breasts were crushed against an unyielding chest, one sinewy leg was trapped between her thighs and a large warm hand wedged under her arm. The strong, fast beat of another heart pounded against her own, racing out of control, her breath mingling with someone else's warm breath.

"Are you all right?" The husky voice, as deep as the velvety darkness, sent a shudder through her, galvanizing her into action.

She sprang away from him, pushing against the hard muscles she could feel flexing in his chest.

"Damn it." At his muffled groan she realized that, in her panic, her knee had dug hard on his groin. She felt him roll to the side, his breathing harsh and labored.

"I'm sorry, are you all right?" Kneeling in the cold ooze by his feet, she reached out blindly in the dark, encountered bunched muscles and immediately drew her hands back.

"I will be. In about ten minutes." He bit off the words tersely, as if he were holding his breath.

"I'm so sorry. Is there anything I can do to help?"

"You've got to be kidding."

The mockery in his strangled voice made her realize what she had said. *Oh, Lord. Of all the stupid things.*

"Who are you?" But she had already recognized the famous voice. It had just taken a while to sink in through her shock and mortification.

"I'm Sam Cooper. Who are you?"

"I'm Emma Jordan."

There was a long pause, then she heard the rustle of movement and a squelching sound.

When his warm breath fanned her face she realized he had also gotten to his knees and was only inches away from her in the dark. And when he spoke his voice rippled with a quiet menace that sent a small shiver through her scalp.

"Oh . . . You are, are you?"

2

"THERE IS A GOD after all," he muttered. "I wanted you and he delivered you into my lap."

"What?" Her hearing must have been knocked out of sync by the fall.

"I was just imagining the pleasure it would give me to get my hands around your throat and wring your neck."

"I beg your pardon!" With a gasp, she automatically clutched a sticky hand to her throat and scrambled to her feet. Just because he was a famous movie star didn't mean he couldn't be a psychotic nut case.

"Listen, lady, I've suffered about as much as I'm going to take on account of you." His angry voice followed her in the darkness as she backed away, until she felt the rough boards pressing against her spine.

"I don't know what you're talking about!" Even she could hear the fear in her voice.

"Then you must be pretty stupid."

He had come closer. Blinded by the dark, every other sense became piercingly acute. She could feel his warmth, smell his foreign male scent.

His voice dropped to a low, intimidating growl. "What do you think I'm doing in this pit?"

His closeness was suffocating. "That's what I was going to ask you!"

She heard him exhale with a sharp hiss. "Don't push your luck. And you can forget the sarcasm, because you're stuck with me in this hole and even Igor at the gate won't hear you scream."

A shiver of fear made her mouth go dry. He was absolutely right. And this man was clearly not sane. His obsessive persistence in going after the screenplay should have rung a warning bell.

"That's what you think. He's due to make his rounds any time now." Would he see through the lie? She couldn't let him sense her fear, even though the darkness was alive with it, and filled with the sound of his breathing. She'd read about nut cases like him, how they thrived on the fear of their victims.·

"That's the first piece of good news I've heard all day."

To her surprise he moved back. She could feel the heat of his body receding, smell once again the sharp odor of damp earth, instead of the warm male scent that was so intimidating in the dark.

She let out a careful sigh of relief. If he was planning on murder, Fritz's imminent arrival would hardly make him happy. He'd obviously been very angry and expressed himself in the extravagant, theatrical way that must be typical of show-business people. But it certainly wasn't the way she was used to being spoken to. If he did it again she'd tell him so.

And she might have that opportunity when it became obvious that Fritz wasn't going to appear. With a sinking heart she looked up to the rim, so very high above her head.

"So tell me, is this how you catch your dinner?"

"What?"

"Do you let your victims lie around here for a while until they're good and dead, or do you like them warm and kicking when you dig in?"

"What are you talking about?"

Oh, God, she really was trapped in here with a madman. She pressed herself into the boards as a cold shiver crept up her spine. But he sounded so normal. A little mocking. Amused, maybe, but normal.

"I read your book, remember," came the deep voice from the inky darkness. "I expected you'd turn out to be some kind of weirdo. A cross between Morticia Addams and the Medusa. And boy, was I right."

Emma gulped for air, struck speechless as the paralyzing fear was overtaken by growing indignation. She pushed herself fiercely away from the wall, only to fall against him. Just as quickly, she pushed herself away again, bracing her hands on his chest, solid and warm under the slippery coating of mud.

"*Me*, a weirdo? That's like the pot calling the kettle black. How dare you be so insulting!"

A low, mirthless chuckle echoed in the gloom. "The lady is insulted." The sarcasm in his husky voice made her bristle, but he continued, his words clipped and hard. "While we're on the subject of insults . . . I'll have you know that I didn't take too kindly to your opinion that I'm just a dumb stud who wouldn't know what to do with your . . . literary masterpiece."

Stunned and indignant, she sucked in her breath. "I never said anything of the sort."

"No? Well, that agent of yours made it quite clear that you think I'll turn it into a piece of B-movie schlock. Your work's no better than anything *I* do. It's entertainment, that's all."

He took the wind abruptly out of her sails. She *had* thought that, and she was still worried about him ruining her creation. But she could hardly say so. Not right now, anyway, while she was stuck here, virtually at his mercy. Even if he probably wasn't a homicidal maniac.

"Look—" she tried to sound patient and rational "—shouldn't we try and find a way out of here instead of wasting our time bickering?"

"I thought you said Igor would be coming around soon." His husky drawl oozed contempt.

"For God's sake, stop calling him Igor! His name is Fritz, and obviously he's not." She took a deep breath, then muttered, "I said that because you frightened me."

He made no immediate response to her admission. There was only a lengthening breathy silence, suddenly pierced by the clear, haunting call of the loon.

Then his low, mocking voice came to her, laced with a hint of malice. "Console yourself with the thought that I wanted to do more."

She was fed up with his bullying. "Look, I'm sorry you fell into this hole, but it was an accident. Sue me if you want, but stop threatening me with violence you have no intention of carrying out."

"You're very sure of me, aren't you?"

He came closer. Once again the heat of his body and his warm musky scent overpowered her, even mingled as they were with the acrid smell of dank mud. His proximity disturbed her, but she wasn't afraid anymore. Sam Cooper was angry, but he wasn't crazy.

"The only thing I'm sure of is that I want to get out of this damn pit!" She turned toward the side and began running her hands over the rough planks. "I don't suppose you've done anything about trying to get out."

"No. I've just been sitting here waiting for you to fall on top of me."

She ignored him. "There's only one way. I'll have to get on your shoulders and climb out. Then I can get a ladder and lower it down to you."

"Why not? You've tromped all over me in every other way. You might as well do it literally."

"I have done no such thing!" There was something disorienting about yelling her indignation into the faceless dark. "You can't say things like that about me!"

"Listen, lady, I can say anything I damn well want. I spent months jumping through hoops just to option your book. I crossed the continent, then drove two hours to finally get here, only to have Igor at the gate scare the hell out of me. And then top it all off by falling into your pit!"

"His name is *Fritz!*" As if it made any difference. "I'm sure he didn't try to frighten you. He wouldn't hurt a fly. It's not my fault if you're so easily intimidated. And as far as your difficulty in optioning my book, none of that would have happened if you'd only learned to take no for an answer! I said I wasn't interested."

"Oh yeah. Good ploy. Keep on saying you're not interested—until the price is right. I've seen it all before. Come on, get on my shoulders." His harsh impatient voice sounded from somewhere around her knees.

"That's not true! I'd never do anything so . . . so manipulative." She made no move to touch him, speechless at the accusation.

"That's your story and you're sticking to it, huh? Come on, come on. . . . I don't want to crouch here all night."

Emma ground her teeth together, trying to stifle the urge to reach out and hit him. "I'm with you there. I've had about as much of your company as I can stand." Reaching out to locate him, her fingers suddenly curved around a hard, muscular shoulder. She flinched at the bodily contact. "As a matter of fact, when we do get out of here, you can get into your car and leave, tonight. I'd sooner work with a pit viper than you."

His hand curled around her wrist in a tight, cruel grip and hauled her toward him. Pulled off-balance, she stumbled and fell against his broad back, then righted herself immediately, as if he were made of hot coals.

"Let me tell *you* something, lady. You can dig as many pits as you want. Never mind Igor, you can have Frankenstein and the Wolfman at your gate, but you've got a written agreement with me to write this screenplay and you're damn well going to do it!"

He still had hold of her wrist in a painful grip.

"Let go of me right now!"

"Get on my shoulders."

Gritting her teeth so hard that her jaw hurt, Emma did what he said and straddled him. As he rose unsteadily to his feet the unfamiliar feel of his warmth between her thighs, the intimacy of their positions, sent a strange shiver trickling down her legs.

Clutching at his head to steady herself, her fingers sank into short, damp hair. The movement brought her crotch hard against the back of his neck. He flexed his shoulders and turned his head from side to side, settling her weight more evenly, rubbing against her as he moved his neck back and forth. Instinctively, her muscles clenched with a jolt of sensation that shocked her.

"You know, holding out like that was very clever—all that high-minded worrying about what Hollywood would do to your precious story. Well, it worked, didn't it? You walked away with all the marbles. You got the money, you got to collaborate on the screenplay *and* you got final approval."

She instantly forgot the stirrings between her thighs. He made her sound like a cold, calculating bitch. As if she'd been deliberately stringing him along.

She wasn't about to tell him the negotiations were all Petra's doing. After all, her agent had worked hard looking out for her best interests. And if he didn't like the terms, he didn't have to agree to them, did he? But now was not the time to argue.

"Do you want to get out of here, or not?" she asked with strained patience.

"What I'd like to do is against the law," he said through gritted teeth. "But I'll settle for getting out of here."

"I think you're the rudest, most bad-tempered person I've ever met in my life." Emma struggled breathlessly to stand on his shoulders, uncaring of any pain she might be inflicting.

"You've lived a very sheltered life, then, haven't you," he grunted, straining with the effort of supporting her.

"Not sheltered enough." She deliberately put one slimy, mud-coated tennis shoe on the top of his head. *I hope this hurts.* "And I sincerely hope we can get this thing written as soon as possible."

"Right now I don't care about getting this thing written. Just get your damn foot off my head."

"Stop being such a wimp. I'm almost there."

Hampered by the cold, slick mud now coating almost every inch of her body, she struggled to grasp at the top of the wood plank wall. Her foot slipped and caught on his ear. He spat out a pungent expletive.

"Swearing at me is not going to get us out of here."

"No. But it does wonders for my frustration."

Now, at least, she could see something besides pitch-black—the big dim shape of the house and the dark trees against the starlit sky.

"Is this how you always treat the people you work with?" she gasped, curling her fingers around the edge of the rough lumber.

"Only the ones who are incompetent."

"Well, that's not me. I know what I'm doing."

He gripped her ankles to steady her and his voice sounded strained. "Yeah? Well, you'd better know what the hell you're doing. Writing a novel is a far cry from writing a screenplay."

He'd just put his finger on her painful misgivings, but she'd be damned if she'd let him know it.

"Don't worry about me," she yelled down at him. "As far as I'm concerned, if we can get this thing done in two weeks or three weeks, instead of six, I'll be thrilled."

Going up on tiptoe on his shoulders she strained forward, trying to reach something solid to hang on to. Her hands scrabbled in the grass, then caught hold of a sturdy tree root protruding from the soil.

"Oh, no, you don't!" he growled. She could feel him shifting beneath her, trying to maintain his balance. "You're not going to rush this just to get rid of me."

Finally she succeeded in hauling herself out and lay on the grass for a moment, panting from the exertion. "Watch me."

"Everything I have is sunk into this project. You're not going to screw it up for me." His deep voice echoed from below. "We work until *I'm* satisfied."

The damp grass felt cool and fresh against her cheek. She wanted to lie there a minute and get her breath, but she forced herself to rise. "I'd be willing to work around the clock just to get you and this screenplay out of here as soon as possible."

Reaching her feet, Emma looked down into the hole and saw nothing but blackness.

"Well? What are you waiting for?" he yelled up from the void. "Go get a ladder."

"I'm really tempted to leave you there all night," she said. "I really am. And if I were half the bitch you seem to think I am, I'd do it."

She stalked off toward the shed, but his voice pursued her. "Hey, Godzilla . . . don't do me any favors."

She scowled and kept going. Who did that man think he was!

Returning with a propane lantern and a small aluminum ladder, she dropped the ladder unceremoniously into the hole and heard a thunk, then a muffled squelch.

"Ow! You hit me. You did that on purpose!"

"I did not." But she couldn't restrain a tiny smirk of malicious pleasure as she pumped up the lantern, lit it and held it up to light his way as he climbed out.

From his thickly matted head to his running shoes Sam Cooper was caked in filthy, slimy gray mud. When he was finally standing beside her he slowly looked himself over and she felt all her anger ebbing away. Suddenly she was stricken with guilt.

"I really am very sorry about this . . . unfortunate accident. I'm sorry you fell in my pit." Feeling sickeningly responsible, she bit her lower lip and tasted grit.

Slowly he raised his head to look at her and a tiny gasp escaped her lips. In his muddied face his eyes were a piercing, startling blue, framed by long, spiky dark lashes. Keen and mocking and filled with accusation. "Just tell me it wasn't a grave."

"Of course, it wasn't a grave! My septic tank needed repair. The crew had to rush off for an . . . emergency. . . ." Her voice petered out under his probing gaze, waiting for the inevitable caustic comment.

"You know it was a stupid thing to do, leaving a gaping hole like that." But his voice was only gently admonishing, as if he were speaking to a very small, rather dim child.

She shrugged, disarmed by this unexpected gentleness. "There wasn't supposed to be anyone here to fall into it. And it's being filled in tomorrow morning."

"Had you forgotten I was coming?"

"I wasn't expecting you until tomorrow evening."

His disconcerting blue gaze remained fixed on her face. This wasn't supposed to be happening. The reason she had wanted to work here was because she would have home-ground advantage. But even in his disheveled state, there was something commanding and powerful about this man that made her feel uneasy and deeply vulnerable.

"Oh, I see." He spoke softly, but with a wealth of meaning that she didn't understand. Then he half turned away from her with a soft, deep chuckle, rubbing the nape of his neck in a tired gesture.

She allowed her gaze to wander over him. It was an odd, disorienting feeling, being in the presence of a celebrity. A familiar stranger.

The famous face was of course completely obscured by grime. He wasn't very much taller than her—about five-ten or -eleven, she guessed—but his compact, broad-shouldered body radiated physical strength and assurance. She already had startling memories of coming into contact with hard muscles in the dark. She felt herself go hot with mortification and bent over to retrieve the ladder from the hole.

"Before we go any farther, you don't have any other pits, bear traps or lurking monsters I should know about, do you?"

"No. I don't." One moment of gentleness was no reason to believe he was anything other than an obnoxious, overbearing legend in his own mind.

"One more thing. Do you have a pet bat?"

Her head jerked up as she let the ladder drop, paying no attention to the clatter as it banged against the wooden sides of the excavation.

"Maybe that passes for humor where you come from, but up here it's just downright rude."

"You're too sensitive. It was an idle question."

"It was nothing of the sort. It was sly innuendo, suggesting that I'm some sort of vampire!"

"If the shoe fits." Through the coating of mud, he gave her a hard, cool look.

"What do you mean?"

"You sucked *me* dry, you and that agent of yours."

The injustice of it made her seethe. "*You're* the one who persisted. You're the one who couldn't take no for an answer!"

"Yes, and you'd be wise to remember that. I always get what I want."

"No matter what it costs. No matter who gets destroyed in the process."

He laughed. "Do you have to be so melodramatic?" He was so untouched, so callous.

Oh yes, she knew that kind of man. She'd been betrayed by that kind of selfish pursuit once. She wasn't going to be a victim again.

"You know, I was just thinking." She gave him a barbed smile. "It's true what they say about famous people. In person they're always shorter than you expect them to be. And you're no exception."

"Listen here, lady, I'm tall where it counts," he drawled, his voice low and husky and suggestive.

She sucked in her breath. "Stop calling me lady! My name is Emma. And you're disgusting!"

He chuckled softly, with a toying hint of intimacy. "It's your mind that's disgusting. You should get it out of the gutter. I was talking about my intellect."

She let out an exasperated sigh and met the keen satirical expression in his eyes. "Look, this is stupid. Let's agree we consider each other a major pain in the rear end, but as you say, we're committed to doing this. Let's just do it. We don't have to like each other."

"That's fine by me. I'll keep my part of the bargain and you keep yours. And you'd better know what you're doing, because if you're wasting my time . . ."

"I can do without your threats, Mr. Cooper. I get the message."

If he'd only been normal and nice she would probably have admitted her nervousness. What did she know about collaborating with anyone, never mind writing a screenplay?

But he wasn't nice. He was absolutely horrible. This was going to be much worse than she'd feared. He hadn't gotten his way and now he was hell-bent on making her pay for it.

"I'll show you where you're going to stay." She turned away in the direction of the guest cottage, her mouth tight with resentment.

"Wait a minute. Aren't I going to stay there?" He pointed back toward the house.

"No. I thought you'd prefer your privacy, so I had the guest house prepared for you."

"That was . . . very considerate of you."

The irony in his smiling voice made her want to push him back into the pit, but she kept walking, rigid with annoyance. She wouldn't let his sarcasm goad her. Before Sam Cooper arrived she had felt badly about inconveniencing him, but now? He expected a cast-iron bitch and he was going to get one.

And, after all, she did have control. She'd been fully prepared to bow to his superior knowledge of the film business. Now, however, she intended to exercise that control to its fullest. She wouldn't cut him one inch of slack.

As she led him through the trees toward the small A-frame near the tip of the point, another bat swooped just overhead in the twilight. Sam made a quick reflexive duck and tripped over a tree root at the same time. Instinctively, Emma reached out to steady him.

"Nervous?" Her fingers closed around his arm—around hard, warm, muscled flesh. She drew away from the disturbing intimacy.

"Very funny," he said through gritted teeth.

"You'll get used to them. They're not pets, but I do enjoy having my little friends around."

He only gave a faint, unamused grunt. "Don't tell me. Northern humor, right?"

Her smile broadened. He wasn't so tough. She could get her digs in. It made her feel a little more equal to the challenge.

Reaching the A-frame, she led him up the steps to the wooden deck. "This is it. I hope you'll be comfortable here." At this point she didn't give a damn whether he was comfortable or not.

Turning the knob, she pushed the door open and reached in to flick a switch, flooding the room with soft light. But he made no move to enter; instead he looked down to the boards at his feet, then cocked her a questioning eyebrow and she knew he was wondering about the slap of the waves in the boathouse underneath.

"Don't worry. You won't end up in Georgian Bay. That only happened once and it was an *extremely* bad summer storm. On a night very much like tonight, actually. Hot and humid." She gave him a guileless smile. With any luck that thought would keep him awake all night.

"Thank you for the reassurance," he said dryly.

"You're welcome."

After shooting her a brief, slightly amused look, he walked in, took a slow, sweeping survey of the living area and the stairs leading up to the loft bedroom, then turned to her. "This is very nice. Thank you."

He was actually sincere. For the first time since they'd met there was no trace of anger or mockery in his voice. His sincerity made her feel ashamed of her ungraciousness. After all, he was her guest and she hadn't been raised to be mean and inhospitable.

"You're welcome." Her voice husky with self-consciousness, she found herself saying, "If you're hungry, come up to the house when you're ready and I'll fix you something to eat."

"Thanks. I'd appreciate that." Under the muck she discerned a small, tired smile.

Emma nodded and abruptly turned away. She headed back down the steps, unable to shake the insidious uneasiness. After all, what did she know about this man? Nothing. And yet she was committed to spending six weeks with him, alone except for Fritz. Granted, the bizarre circumstances of their meeting didn't help, but this man had the most shocking effect on her behavior.

Entering the house through the mudroom off the kitchen, she flicked on the outdoor lights and made a face at the grubby fingerprints she left behind on the switch plate. God forbid the man should fall back in the hole.

Kicking off her mud-encrusted tennis shoes, she headed upstairs to shower. The drying mud felt stiff and sticky on her bare legs and was already tightening on her face.

This was *never* going to work. Before Sam Cooper arrived she'd been worried enough about working with a stranger. But now she knew for sure it would be impossible. Because, on top of everything else, he *hated* her. And for some reason that knowledge hurt. But he was never going to know it. She wouldn't spend a single second with him that was not filled by work.

Cool, aloof and professional. That's how she would play it from here on in.

SAM KNOCKED on the front door for the second time that evening, and waited. Again, the house lay silent. Now, however, lights burned in the hall beyond the lace-curtained glass and in the bay windows flanking the door.

After a moment he tried the doorknob and to his surprise it turned. Had the door been unlocked all along? Was that all he had to do, open it and walk in? Could he have saved himself all that humiliation and fury?

He stepped into the front hall. French doors opened into the rooms on either side and a broad staircase on one wall led to the upper floor.

"Hello," he called out. The word fell into the silence. *The silence of the tomb.* "Stop that," he muttered to himself.

He'd seen enough of Emma Jordan, even covered in drying, cracking mud, to know that, whatever she might be, she was obviously no wacko. She'd been indignant and outraged, with just the right touch of arrogance.

His instinctive judgment had been right. She didn't have her head in the clouds while her agent did the dirty work. She was a sharp, shrewd operator, tough as nails. She and Petra made a good team, playing that intimidating little game of inaccessibility. It wasn't that he hadn't offered to pay handsomely for the rights; she had wanted it all. She had him by the balls and she knew it.

"Where are you? It's me, Sam." He walked to the foot of the stairs. "Miss Jordan?"

"Mr. Cooper. Hi." He peered up the stairwell, but in the soft light of the hall-table lamp all he could make out was the glimmer of a white robe in the shadows above. "Go into the living room," she called down. "I'll be right there."

That voice. There was something about it—deep for a woman, with a velvety roughness that had made the hairs on his arms stand on end when he'd first heard it in the darkness of the pit. A voice that could make her a lot of money in his business.

"Take your time." He strolled through the open French doors on his right into a spacious, high-ceilinged living room.

The room surprised him. Light and airy; all calm, sophisticated pastels without being in the least cold or unwelcoming. A pleasing mix of old and new with touches of sumptuous luxury, like the peach leather sofa and pastel wool Persian rugs on polished oak boards the color of honey.

The kind of eclectic, comfortable room that spelled home, not the work of some expensive decorator.

A van Gogh print hung on one wall, next to a framed poster of Fred Astaire in midstep, coattails flying. Above the fireplace and on the wall by the window, hung original oils and watercolor landscapes by an artist he didn't know, but whoever he was, he was damn good.

Okay, so she had taste.

And she loved to read. No surprise there. He wandered over to one of the floor-to-ceiling built-in shelves that flanked the French doors and ran a finger over the packed rows of books. Chekhov's plays, a fat book on organic gardening, an old and battered copy of *Pride and Prejudice* next to a leather-bound collection of Evelyn Waugh.

Okay, so she was widely read. No reason to start feeling intimidated. He'd read a few books himself.

In front of the couch stood a round glass coffee table, supported by the white marble capital of a Corinthian column. On top lay a stack of magazines.

"Hello . . . what do we have here?"

He stooped to pick up the top copy. His own face stared back at him from the cover of *Vanity Fair*. And also from *People*, the next in the stack. With one finger he flicked through the collection, each progressively more tawdry, until he reached the bottom to find the final publication, almost two years old and graced with an obviously doctored picture that featured a black lace bra dangling from his teeth.

He had to smile at that one, remembering Robyn's helpless squeals of laughter, and how they'd taken turns reading the article out loud to each other, naked and cross-legged on the rumpled bed. A little later they had made love. She had felt so warm and wonderful in his arms, the memory still filled him with bittersweet joy, despite the ache of emptiness. He didn't know it was to be the last time like that for them. The last time he would make love to her.

With a sigh he shook his head, then focused again on the magazines in his hand. So this was what Emma Jordan based her judgment of him on. He dropped them back on the coffee table with a spurt of cynicism. Nice to know the intellectual Miss Jordan wasn't above dipping into a little trash.

As he straightened he noticed the lacy white cotton cardigan slung carelessly over the back of a tapestry-covered wing chair. Well, she was no neat freak. He hooked it up with one finger and got a faint whiff of a light, fresh fragrance. Lifting it closer to his face, he inhaled deeply, then frowned. There was something pure and innocent about that smell. All flowers and sunshine and fresh air.

Her voice had the depth and assurance of an older woman, but this clean, young scent said something different. That, and the way she had felt. Lush, firm . . . youthful.

He couldn't erase the sensation of her body pressed against his in the dark. The voluptuous weight of her full breasts crushed against his chest, the way her hips had fit against his so perfectly. Until her knee made agonizing contact with his groin it had felt . . . familiar. Disturbingly familiar. And bizarre.

As bizarre as everything else connected with this woman.

Who was Emma Jordan? Intelligent, well-read, a woman of excellent taste. That much he had easily deduced. Clearly much younger than he had originally thought. A hard-headed businesswoman, for sure. Except for that moment in the pit, when she'd betrayed her fear and vulnerability to him. That had brought him up short.

The memory carried a twinge of guilt. He had deliberately played on her fear. But, damn it, he'd had a right to his anger and resentment. And after all she'd put him through, a little revenge had tasted sweet.

Okay, enough guilt. He dropped the cardigan back onto the chair. But he still didn't have a clear picture of this woman. Nothing added up. And if she wasn't the occult weirdo, either, then who was she?

A slow insidious tingling spread up the back of his neck, as if there were someone, some *presence*, standing behind him. Boy, that woman still had him spooked.

To prove to himself that he was still being a jerk, he turned and for the second time that evening his heart slammed into his chest like an express train. His jaw fell so hard he could swear he actually felt it hit the wide oak boards, and his eyes started from their sockets as if they were on springs, like a damned cartoon character.

But he couldn't help it, as he stood gawking at the figure silently watching him from the doorway.

3

"I'M SORRY. I didn't mean to startle you, Mr. Cooper."

"Startle me?" The pent-up breath rushed out in laughter that had relief written all over it to an embarrassing degree. But what was the point in trying to cover it up? "Stunned would be closer to the truth."

This was his Mary Shelley? His eccentric old recluse? He couldn't take his eyes off her, couldn't believe what he was seeing.

"Oh dear, this doesn't seem to be your day."

Was there really a hint of mockery in her voice, or was his judgment thrown by the sight of her? Framed by a cloud of dark chestnut curls, even completely bare of make-up, her finely modeled oval face had the porcelain perfection of an antique cameo.

"Don't worry, I needed the jolt. After all, it's been forty-five minutes since anything weird has happened. I was beginning to feel a sense of anticlimax." This would teach him for thinking in stereotypes.

She only gave him a cool smile that didn't touch her eyes. "Oh, good. I wouldn't want to disappoint you. After all, you are my guest." The condescension in her tone stung.

"Such hospitality. I'm overwhelmed."

"It could be the heat. And you have had a long and..." She hesitated delicately and deliberately. "A long and *trying* day."

Even barefoot, in a loose, unassuming black cotton T-dress, she still radiated aloof, patrician elegance from every inch of her tall, slender frame. As she walked slowly toward him he caught the hint of a superior smile. No doubt she found it very amusing to see him struggling in her web.

"You don't have to condescend to me," he said, a shade too sharply. "We both know I fell in a damn pit."

He unclenched his jaw. This was no time to practice his Kirk Douglas. He wasn't normally so touchy. Why was he allowing this woman to get to him?

Between the dark winged brows a tiny crease appeared. "I was hoping we wouldn't have to relive that whole fiasco."

"We don't have to relive it." Maybe it was the unsettling way she seemed to look right through him. Especially when he couldn't tell what was happening behind those deep-set eyes, the indefinable color of smoke. "But you don't have to tiptoe around it, either."

"I wasn't tiptoeing around it. I was merely being polite, and so far it hasn't been easy." She tightened her mouth in annoyance, her lips full and rosy pink against the creamy paleness of her skin. No lipstick, he noticed. So much nicer to kiss unpainted lips.

Whoa. Wait a minute. Kissing? No, there'd be no kissing. No doubt about that. If his long-dormant sex drive had to rear its ugly head, it had picked a hell of a time to do it. And a woman who couldn't be more *wrong* for the part. He rubbed at the nape of his neck and gave a small wry laugh.

"What are you laughing at?"

"Me."

"And what on earth is that supposed to mean?" Her cool disdain was only emphasized by the high, slanting cheekbones and lush mouth that gave her an exotic allure. A darkly mysterious hothouse bloom.

"Now I understand the source of your arrogance."

She started, indignation making her cheekbones pink. "My arrogance!"

"Like all other beautiful women, you think you can get whatever you want."

"Of all the—"

"Well, not from me. I don't play those kinds of games. They don't interest me. When all is said and done, you're just another pretty face, and I see plenty of those in my line of work."

He knew only too well how insignificant and superficial appearances could be. Emma Jordan might appear to be a gorgeous, fragile butterfly, but her wings were pure steel.

"Are you quite through?" She was shaking with indignation and something else that caused a sick feeling in her stomach. "I am not going to spend the next six weeks sparring with you, so from now on keep your primitive attempts at psychoanalysis to yourself."

"Gladly, provided you remember the same goes for your contempt."

"Contempt? I have been making every effort to be polite."

He laughed. "Is that what you've been trying to do?" He laughed again and she hated the mocking sound of it. "Here, let me show you how it's done." Now his voice softened to a womanly tone. "Good evening, Sam, I'm sorry I kept you waiting. Sit down, make yourself at home . . . and so on and so on," he finished with a small, mocking bow.

She flinched, feeling hurt. "You've already decided I'm a bitch, haven't you?"

He just looked at her, unmoved. Anger rose inside her and she dredged up some sneering contempt of her own.

"I'll never change your mind, but I have news for you. I don't care. Think what you want." She shrugged. "Your opinion matters exactly this much—" she snapped her fingers "—to me." Lifting her chin defiantly, she willed her mouth not to quiver.

In the soft lamplight his clear blue eyes fixed her with that relentless, probing gaze she'd already begun to hate. Then he came closer, his movements fluid and unhurried, the tight-knit, athletic body that was no pumped-up hulk, but all hard, dense muscle. There was more than a hint of arrogance in the way he stopped, so close she could smell the fresh scent of his soap, and shoved his hands into the pockets of well-worn jeans riding low on his lean hips.

"You have a nice place here."

She blinked and stared at him for a moment, disoriented again. Was this guy schizophrenic? Or were these mercurial changes of mood and topic normal for him? The trouble was she didn't know him, even though they'd been arguing with all the contempt of familiarity.

"Thanks, I like it."

He was a stranger to her, but he seemed so familiar— straight from a magazine cover. The short, soft brown hair, the rugged, handsome face and piercing blue eyes, the slightly crooked nose that had clearly been broken at least once and for which he'd rejected the vanity of cosmetic repair. It all added up to that eminently bankable air of earthy, dependable masculinity that had made him a star.

"It's very warm and welcoming."

Something in her tightened at the sound of his low, husky voice. She couldn't shake her suspicion. Even though he seemed to be offering the proverbial olive branch, his closeness filled her with an uncomfortable tingle of wariness.

"It's home," she said, shrugging. She couldn't let him affect her this way. She was quite capable of keeping him at bay, and she should remember that.

His firm mouth curved upward in a tired smile. If she were in his position she'd be feeling awfully strange and unwelcome. Emma felt a stirring of compassion.

"It's not what I expected."

"What did you expect?"

He grinned wickedly and something in her tightened. "If I tell you, we'll start fighting again."

"Then by all means don't tell me." She wasn't sure his teasing was any easier to take than his antagonism.

"I like it." He nodded his head as he looked around, bemused. "This place really feels like home. I think I'll be very comfortable here."

He turned back to her, his eyes warmed to blue gray in the lamplight, searching hers as if he wanted to reach down inside her; eyes that were too deep, too intimate, too curious. Claustrophobia swept over her again, closing in on her. Sam Cooper was here to get what he wanted at any cost.

It was time to make him aware of the parameters, so there would be no confusion. She didn't want to be responsible for his entertainment, or anything else beyond seeing that his basic needs were met.

For ten years she had willingly played the perfect hostess. But those days were gone. That had been another part of her life. And she had been a very different person. "Look, Mr. Cooper—"

"Call me Sam," he interrupted, with a small coaxing smile.

She'd seen that smile on-screen. The kind of smile that could charm the birds from the trees. Part of his appeal, no doubt.

"Look, Sam, I think it would be best if we laid out a few ground rules, don't you?"

"Whatever you say." He sounded reasonable, but she saw the wary glint in his eyes.

Well, there was only one way to say it. "This is my home and I like my privacy. Your cabin is completely self-sufficient and apart from my office, there is no reason why... There is no reason for you—"

"To invade your privacy? Is that what you're trying to say, Emma?"

She noticed his use of her first name and the small ironic smile accompanying it. Taking a deep breath, she let it out. "Yes, that's what I'm trying to say. Under the circumstances I'm sure you'll appreciate your privacy, too."

"Oh, undoubtedly. Thank you for being so perceptive."

The words mocked her, even if his tone did sound sincere, but she let it go. After all, she deserved his sarcasm. He was here because she couldn't work anywhere else. But now that he knew her expectations, surely things would go a lot more smoothly and she'd be able to handle him being here much more easily.

"I promised you supper. What can I get you?" With that awkward necessity off her chest, she was anxious to feed the man and send him on his way.

"Anything at all, I don't want to be a bother." His smile was genuine, but the satirical glimmer in his eyes did nothing to put her at ease. "However, I won't say no to an ice-cold drink to start."

"Beer?"

"You read my mind."

I wish! Never before had she met a man whose sheer presence was so intrusive, so tangible. Almost suffocating.

She turned and escaped the room. It had been bad enough in the blackness of the pit, with only that gravelly voice and a mental picture to deal with. It was far worse face-to-face.

And all her research didn't help. Being able to minutely dissect his appeal didn't dissipate one iota of the overpowering vitality he radiated. Women didn't line up around the block for his movies just to admire the escalating firepower of his arsenal.

Heading into the farmhouse kitchen, she went straight to the fridge and got out a beer. She turned to find him standing in the doorway, watching her. He must have moved with the quiet stealth of a cat.

"Can I help?" His eyes followed her in that compelling way, as if he were privy to her inner turmoil.

"That isn't necessary, I can manage." No, it wasn't just her imagination making her anxious. There was something predatory about this man. That was the word, *predatory.*

Intensely conscious of his gaze on her back, she stepped over to the cupboard and reached up to get a beer mug from the top shelf.

"Allow me," he murmured.

His warm breath grazed her ear and she shuddered as a hand reached up beyond hers for the mug. She hadn't even heard him come up behind her. The heat of his body, so close but not touching, burned all along hers and the disturbing smell of male evoked sharp, shocking memories.

After two years of living in her solitary world she'd forgotten that physical essence of a man. Well, she'd better get used to it again. There would be no escape for the next six weeks.

Handing him the beer she still held, Emma walked back across the kitchen and opened the fridge. "What would you like to eat?"

"Whatever you're having."

"I've already had my dinner. I hope you don't mind eating alone?"

"A sandwich will be fine, then. I'm really not all that hungry. Must be the heat."

She tensed at the deep voice much too close behind her. Slamming the door shut, she tried to master her racing heart and rally her spirit as she turned to face him. Once again, she felt trapped, overwhelmed by that closed-in feeling.

"If you're just trying to be polite, it's not necessary. I don't mind making you a meal. It's the least I can do."

She wrapped her arms across her body, feeling miserably strange and uneasy in her own kitchen, and all because of this man. Sam Cooper didn't hesitate to barge in where angels feared to tread, to bend everyone and everything to *his* will.

"After I fell in your pit, you mean?"

She shot him a quick look, but he was smiling without rancor and this time she knew he was teasing her. It should have made her feel more relaxed, but it didn't. No smile had ever filled her with more trepidation.

They had a shared past now. An anecdote to recall. As if they were friends. And once again the trapped feeling closed in on her. She didn't want to let anyone that close, especially him. He made her feel as if he could look right inside her and take her apart.

"It seems I have a whole list of offenses to atone for." She attempted a smile. A remnant of her earlier self came to her aid; the mistress of light social chitchat.

"The list of my sins is probably even longer. What do you say we wipe both slates clean?"

She nodded and smiled, feeling intensely awkward. They hadn't even started yet and it already impossible. What had Petra got her into? More to the point, how was she going to get through it?

He was still too close, but she lifted her gaze to look squarely in those brilliant blue eyes and hold their probing intensity without flinching.

"What kind of sandwich would you like?"

"I don't care, anything is fine."

"If you'll have a seat, I'll make you one." She started to turn away, but he stopped her with a hand on her arm.

"You don't have to wait on me, Emma. I can make my own sandwich." He must have felt the fine tremors of alarm racing over her skin, but his steady expression gave nothing away.

"Why don't you do that." She stepped away and he let go. The urge to turn and run was overwhelming, but she fought it down. Somehow, though, she had to get away. "Just help yourself to whatever you need. I'm going for a quick dip, then I'm turning in. We'll talk further tomorrow."

Even though his grip had been gentle, she automatically rubbed at the spot where he had held her, trying to erase the residual tingling of his warm hand on her flesh.

"What time would you like to get started in the morning?" He watched her, his gaze still penetrating but a little baffled.

"Is eight all right for you?" she suggested.

"Perfect."

With a small nod she started to turn away, then an unwelcome thought came to her. "Your fridge isn't stocked yet. Fritz will do that tomorrow...."

"What happened to him?"

She took a deep breath. It was inevitable he would ask, but she didn't want to say anymore than was necessary. "A car accident. He was badly burned."

"What about plastic surgery? Surely something can be done for the poor guy."

"They're working on it. You should have seen him before." She edged toward the doorway. "Anyway, as I was saying, there's no food in your fridge so you're welcome to come over for breakfast."

"Thanks, that's very kind of you." He nodded and his mouth curved in a smile that held a disturbing mixture of vulnerability and virility.

"Good night." Dashing out of the room, Emma took the stairs two at a time to her bedroom.

She slipped into her bathing suit and put the cotton dress back on over it, then made her way downstairs again. Passing through the kitchen, she saw that he had all the fixings for a sandwich spread across the counter and was busy buttering the bread. He glanced up when she entered, but only shot her a keen look and a silent wave of the hand holding the knife as she hurried toward the back door.

It didn't take him long to make himself at home, Emma thought wryly as she let herself out into the hot night air. In a strange way it made her feel slightly reassured. At least he was comfortable looking after himself.

In the sultry darkness she headed straight down to the water and waded in. There was some consolation in the thought that he would no doubt find the country solitude much too quiet and spend his free time looking for the kind of excitement he was used to. Fortunately Toronto was only a couple of hours away.

Judging by his media coverage, his favored pastimes included everything from para-sailing at an exclusive Mexican resort to going on photo safaris in Kenya.

The water felt deliciously cool and refreshing as she floated on her back and looked up at the half-moon riding the velvety depths of the starry sky. She didn't usually read the gossip magazines, but the prospect of this stranger coming to work at her home had prompted thorough research.

Born on a Montana cattle ranch, Sam Cooper fell into acting when he was supposedly "discovered" while delivering horses to a movie set, or some such far-fetched romantic nonsense.

When he'd first gone to Los Angeles his name had been linked with more than the usual parade of starlets. Now, having met him and felt the force of that maverick, untamable masculinity, she could understand why.

He'd married one of those young actresses, Robyn Wyman. In photographs she looked pretty, but was hardly the kind of stunning beauty an ambitious actor might choose to draw attention from the paparazzi. Maybe her appeal had been in her willingness to turn a blind eye to his continual wandering. The poor woman didn't have to cope with it very long. Thirty-six was far too young, and ovarian cancer was a horrible way to go. Even while Robyn lay dying, the stories never abated. But it was no less than Emma expected from a Hollywood marriage.

Not having seen any of his films, she'd rented the six available at Fenelon Falls Video, including his debut, a mindless, badly-written police drama in which he played a street cop on the edge.

The budgets got bigger, the films got better, but even in that first one she could see why he'd made it so big. He had a spark, a charisma that grabbed your attention and never let go every second he was on the screen. He had that spark in person, too.

But she still couldn't understand his interest in *Belial.* Nothing she had seen or read explained why he'd pursue a story so far removed from anything he had ever done and everything he seemed to be.

Suddenly she heard a soft splash, felt a movement of the water around her, then a wet dark head emerged beside her. With a gasp of shock she submerged, swallowed water and surfaced, coughing, as she scrambled away from him to a safe distance.

"I hope you don't mind if I join you? A quick dip before bed sounded like a good idea." Sam smiled and she caught a gleam of white teeth in the pale light of the moon.

"I don't mind at all. As a matter of fact I was just about to get out, so you'll have the water to yourself." She turned in the waist-high water and began wading to shore, but had only gone a couple of paces when his voice made her stop.

"What are you afraid of?"

After the initial shock of his appearance, her heart had slowed its mad hammering, a little, but now began to speed up again, battering against her ribs. *Calm down.* Ruthlessly, she clamped down on the urge to fling herself toward the shore, to escape into the sheltering gloom.

"I'm not afraid of anything."

A dark shape in the moonlit water, he waded closer, the soft liquid swish of his movements unbearably loud in the still, empty night.

Run, a voice inside her whispered. But how could she, after denying her fear?

He was too close to her now in the ghostly light; she could see his smile had vanished. "You talk a brave story, but inside you're afraid."

"Stop saying that! I am not afraid of you." She edged away; his closeness was overwhelming, suffocating.

"I never said you were afraid of *me*." He gave her a searching look. "But while we're on the subject, why do you flinch every time I come near you?"

Her heart gave a painful jolt. He was right. God help her, but he was right. "I don't!"

"You do." He moved closer, not touching but close enough for her to feel the heat of his flesh warming hers, inhale his masculine scent. "What do you think I'm going to do to you?" he asked, his voice low and husky on the soft night air, his warm breath fanning her face.

Frozen to the spot, she couldn't move, her feet only sinking deeper into the sandy lake bottom.

Then, to her relief, he moved a few feet away, with a deep chuckle that held little humor. "Do you think I'm going to attack you? That I pose a sexual threat to you?" There was no smile on his face now as he stood with his hands on his hips, watching her, the water swirling around his thighs.

"Hardly."

He was so far off base that for the first time she began to feel almost comfortable in his presence.

"That's it, isn't it? Well, stop worrying. I'm not interested. The day I have to force a woman to have sex with me is the day you can throw me into your pit and fill it in."

"That's not it." A faint smile tugged at the corners of her mouth.

He thought it was all about sex. Hardly a surprising assumption. After all, he was a handsome and potently masculine man. From what she'd read of his sexual exploits, he had droves of women throwing themselves at him. If he had come to think of himself as irresistible, who could blame him? But sex had nothing to do with her unease. That part of her was long dead.

"Besides, have you forgotten Fritz at the gate? He's all the protection I need."

"Fritz or no Fritz, you don't have to worry about me. I'm only interested in you for one reason and it has nothing to do with sex."

"And I have no idea why we're even having this discussion." She turned away and began wading toward shore.

"Because we're not going to be able to work together if you keep treating me like I've got the plague."

She whirled around to face him. "Look, give me a break. I don't know you from Adam, but from the moment we met you've been rude to me, you tried to frighten me, you've threatened me with violence. Am I supposed to feel comfortable with you?"

"I don't care whether you feel comfortable or not. Get used to me." She heard the threat in his soft voice. "You wanted me here. *You* insisted on the collaboration—"

"*I* insisted?" She cut him off angrily. She felt cornered and defensive. "You held it out as incentive—"

"I did nothing of the sort."

It was becoming clear that Petra hadn't been telling her everything. From all that he'd said so far, it sounded as if her agent had been far more ruthless than she'd ever suspected. But this smacked of outright deception. She couldn't blame him for feeling resentful. She was going to have to call Petra and find out the truth.

But she wasn't about to excuse herself by exposing her agent. She was grateful to Petra for having faith in her work and protecting her privacy, sparing her the usual round of promotion when Petra discovered how distressing she found the prospect. So she'd just have to live with his bad opinion.

"I might be crazy, but I'm not stupid." His face set in hard, determined lines, like granite in the moonlight. Water droplets sparkled on marble skin, on slicked-back hair emphasizing the strong bones of his implacable face. "Okay, you got your way, but you may have ended up with more than you bargained for."

The light carved and sculpted every smoothly muscled curve of an equally hard, powerful body. But it was his expression that sent a small, warning shudder through her.

Now she knew what it was about him that unsettled her. Intensity. Raw ambition. The ruthless desire to get what he wanted, no matter what it cost. Her right to a peaceful life counted for nothing with him. She was an obstacle, pure and simple.

So he thought she'd held out for everything, and won. And now he was going to make her pay for her temerity in opposing him. A surge of anger made her clench her fists.

"This *is* what I bargained for, Mr. Cooper, and this is the way it's going to be. We work together from eight in the morning till five in the evening. The rest of the time there is no need for us to see each other. You have your space and I have mine."

"You think it's going to be that simple? Boy, are you naive."

"Not so naive as to think that you, the king of B-movies, could do anything other than ruin my story."

She saw his face tighten and felt a twinge of satisfaction. That got him where it hurt. His pride. But it wasn't enough; some demon drove her on.

"I mean, what in your experience can prepare you to play a part like Belial? There are no car crashes, no buildings being blown up. Just the complexities of this character on whom the entire story hinges. Everything you've done so far has relied on dazzling special effects to distract the audience from one-dimensional characters trapped in an even thinner plot—"

"Don't say another word." The soft hiss stopped her. Cold, hard anger glittered in his eyes, sharply etched every line of his face. And something else, something that turned her veins to ice. "You've already made two mistakes. I'd hate to see you make a third. It could be fatal."

"What are you talking about?"

"Your first mistake was letting me in here. Your second was not knowing when to shut your luscious little mouth." He drew out the last words with quiet relish, low and evil, in a way that made her feel cheapened and degraded, and very, very frightened.

"My God, you really are mad," she gasped.

But he only smiled. A small, cruel smile. Another man seemed to stand in front of her. And suddenly the night was vast and dark, and she was utterly alone. He came slowly toward her through the water, only ankle-deep near the shore.

"Normally I don't warn them, but I like you." Now he was coaxing, apologetic, exuding the ominous calm that presages an inevitable frenzy of fulfillment.

In cold horror she stumbled backward, away from the low, caressing voice. "You're crazy."

He moved like a striking cobra, one strong, muscled arm pinning her squirming body against his, clamping the other hand over her mouth to cut off the scream of terror. "No. I'm very, very sane. I just enjoy this."

She struggled harder, trying to free her mouth, but his grip tightened.

"Don't even try to scream. I could break your neck so easily." He rotated her head to prove his point, his fingers digging into her cheek with enough pressure to threaten pain, but not really causing it, not yet.

The deadly, pitiless silence of the empty night filled with the sound of his unhurried breathing and her own frantic heartbeats. The man was mad.

"You don't think I know evil," he whispered in her ear, seductive and insinuating. His warm breath grazed her neck, sent small icy shivers trickling down her spine. "You said I was disgusting, but I can make you want me—"

"No."

"Yes . . . I'll prove it."

Still keeping her body prisoner, slowly, tormentingly, he slipped his hand between her legs, his fingers brushing close but not quite touching her. A shocking wave of heat throbbed low in her pelvis. She arched and struggled in his viselike grip, but to no avail; her breasts were crushed against his chest, her thin, wet bathing suit heightening the abrasive friction, with every movement rubbing her pebbled nipples harder against his bare flesh.

But he only pulled her closer, until she felt him pressed against her hip, hard and aroused. "My dear, I am evil."

She felt his hot lips against her ear, then tracing along her jaw, getting closer to her mouth. She tried to jerk her head away, but his arms were like iron bands holding her fast, molding her even more firmly against him. But not even that could still her helpless shuddering.

"And I'll stay here until I get what I want." The wet, slippery bathing suits were no barrier. They might as well be pressed naked against each other. "And what I want is you, body... and soul."

He took her mouth with lips that were remorseless, inexorable. Not a kiss designed to give pleasure, only to abuse. His tongue forced its way into her mouth, thrusting slowly, using her ruthlessly for his own warped amusement. The heat pulsed hotter and hotter inside her, until she thought she'd die from it.

Her head swam, numb with terror. He was unhinged. She was at his mercy. Was she going to die here, at the hands of a psychopath?

Suddenly he let her go, pushing her gently away. The cool night air rushed over skin warmed by his body, raising goose bumps. Unsupported, she swayed.

He reached out to steady her with firm, gentle hands, and a small quirk of his lips. "What do you think? Was that convincing enough for you?"

"Convincing... What do you mean?" Her voice came out in a thready gasp as her head reeled. She shivered, suddenly cold, and backed away toward the shore.

"You had doubts about my acting ability. Still think I'll have trouble playing Belial?"

"You were acting?" She struggled for breath, trying to take it in, as her heart finally began slowing its painful gallop.

For an answer his smile broadened. Nothing like that blood-chilling smile of a few moments before. Belial's demonic smirk. And when he had kissed her, he *was* Belial, aroused by the degradation he was inflicting on her.

Emma strode through the ankle-deep shallows, hauled off and slapped him with every ounce of furious strength she possessed. So hard that her fingers stung with numbness and the shock jolted through her arm right up into her shoulder.

So hard that he rocked back on his heels with the impact. So hard that, even in the weak moonlight, she could see the dark imprint of her hand on his cheek.

Then she turned and walked away.

4

"EMMA!" SAM'S VOICE rang out behind her, sharp and urgent, as he splashed noisily after her through the shallows. "Emma, wait!"

The strength of her anger vanished as a wave of panic rose up, propelling her into a run when her feet touched dry ground. She had to get away. Away from him, away from the shocking, melting heat. Even now, that heat still pulsed strong and rhythmic and painful, deep down inside. But she barely reached the dark mass of the old willow before he caught up and grabbed her arm.

"Please, don't leave like this. I'm sorry." His low, anguished voice hardly registered as he turned her toward him, holding her captive by both arms now.

With all the frightening clarity of a nightmare she saw his face, beautiful, sensual, all angles and shadows in the stark, pale light, every clinging water droplet a tiny moonlit prism on his marble-smooth skin. But all her painful awareness focused on the rough contact of his wet flesh against hers where he gripped her.

"I'm sorry," he murmured again, confused, disturbed. His hands gentled, thumbs moving in minute circles on the soft skin of her upper arms.

Too close to him again, too close. She could smell his heat, and the awful trembling increased until she couldn't catch her breath.

"Let go of me...please," she gasped, trying so hard to keep herself together, not let him see her panic, but it was too late.

"You're shaking. You're afraid of me!" he said incredulously. He took a step closer, his voice low and urgent. "Don't be. I won't hurt you, trust me."

He reached out and curved an arm around her. Cold and clammy with fear, she felt his warm, hard male flesh pulling her against him, enveloping her. Wave after wave of sickness rolled over her, and she began pushing blindly against him.

"Let go of me! Let go of me right now!" She could hear the sharp edge of hysteria as her words reverberated in the moist night air, but she didn't care anymore what he thought, just so long as he stopped touching her.

He moved away, raising his hands in appeasement. "Okay. Okay, I won't touch you. Just calm down."

He frowned, concerned and puzzled, and Emma forced herself to take a deep, slow breath. He was right, she had to calm down. But she couldn't seem to stop the trembling that had taken over her whole body, or fight the unreasoning terror.

"You don't have to fear me. I won't hurt you, I promise," he said quietly, his voice gentle but firm, as if he were speaking to a frightened animal. "Emma, are you listening to me?"

He reached for her and the touch galvanized her into speech as she yanked her hand away. "Yes, yes, I'm listening, I believe you. Now I have to go."

"Wait." He reached for her again, but his hand remained suspended in the air between them, supplicating. "Just give me a chance to explain."

The helpless note in his husky voice sent a wave of prickly awareness washing over her, and she took a shaky step back. The very thought of him touching her again filled her with dread. She didn't want to feel that dangerous, enervating heat.

"You don't have to explain anything. I understand. Please, I just want to go home." She didn't mean to plead, but Sam

Cooper was still blocking her path, still making her feel trapped, and she knew her voice still held the ring of desperation.

He heard it, too. The muscles in his jaw flexed with exasperation. He was trying to be patient, that was obvious, but it was equally obvious that he was finding it difficult.

"You can go any time you want." He let out his breath on an exasperated sigh, and stepped out of the way. "I'm just trying to apologize Emma, that's all. I behaved badly. That was a stupid thing to do. I'm sorry."

He seemed sincere, but clearly confused by the violence of her reaction. He backed away a few paces, and she felt instant relief, but he continued to watch her with steady curiosity. She took a deep breath, filling her lungs with air, like a person confined in a small space for too long.

"Yes, it was a stupid thing to do." Her pounding heart was slowing down now and she began to walk on shaking legs.

He fell into step beside her, stumbling over the dark, uneven ground. "I just figured that I could talk until the cows came home and I'd never convince you that, if nothing else, I can act. But I should have found another way to show you. That was really dumb."

"Yes, it was." At last she felt a little more on top of things, a little less out of control. "Don't you *ever* try anything like that again. I don't like being manhandled." But despite the brave words she quickened her pace. The urge to get away was still very strong.

He kept up with her rapid steps. "You have my solemn promise. Do you believe me?"

"Yes. Yes, I believe you." Through the trees she could see the comforting yellow glow of the porch light outside the kitchen door. All she wanted to do was get home, reach sanctuary.

But he stepped in front of her, forcing her to stop. "You're lying. You're still afraid of me," he insisted. Then the sudden hardness ebbed and a slightly pleading note crept in. "I'll do anything to prove to you that you have no reason to be."

"I'm not afraid of you."

He raised an eyebrow. He didn't believe her. And why should he? She was still shaking like a leaf and her heart was beating fast and furious.

She licked her dry, trembling lips. "You did frighten me back there. I thought you were a psychopathic maniac, but I'm not afraid of you now."

He said nothing for a moment, but kept on looking at her with a steady, probing gaze, as if he could see straight through to the very heart of her fear. "Then why are you still behaving as if I were a deranged killer?" he asked finally.

"I'm not!" She squeezed her eyes shut for a second and forced herself to speak more calmly. "I'm not. I'm just cold and wet and tired. I want to go home, that's all."

He slowly shook his head, unconvinced and curious. "I just don't understand…I don't understand." And something told her that he was the type of man who didn't let go, once his curiosity was aroused.

From somewhere off in the darkness came the unearthly whoop of a nighthawk diving down on its prey. Emma took a lungful of air. "This is never going to work, this collaboration."

He stiffened beside her and she heard his sharp indrawn breath. "Yes, it will. It will work," he insisted earnestly, reaching for her arm once again, his fingers curling around her wrist. "I promise I'll do whatever you want. I'll work any way you want. You won't have any more trouble from me."

With a sharp jerk she pulled her hand away. "To begin with, don't touch me anymore. I don't like it."

"Hey, I've learned my lesson. I won't even *look* at you again. As a matter of fact, I'll go into town right now and buy myself the largest pair of blinkers I can find." He laughed, trying to ease the tension, and hated the phony sound of it. What the hell had he done? What was he doing?

There was no answering laugh, or even a smile. Emma shook her head and looked down. "This is never going to work."

Her face was concealed by a screen of tangled damp curls, but the despair in her voice was clear enough. Unexpectedly it wrenched at his heart.

"Yes, it is. We *can* do this." He was desperate to convince her and he sounded it. But not just because of the script anymore. Suddenly it was important to convince her that she could trust him. That he was a nice guy. He took a steadying breath. "We can do this on whatever terms you want. At one minute past five I'm out of here. You won't see me until the next morning."

"I thought you said I was being naive, that it wouldn't work," she murmured, tremulous and unsure.

"We'll *make* it work. We'll do it any way that's comfortable for you. Let's just get this screenplay done, huh?"

She didn't say anything, just stared past him at the moonlit lake. The silence lengthened and he watched her in that compulsive way he was beginning to hate. But he couldn't seem to stop himself.

Her eyes still looked too large in her face and her skin was creamy and smooth in the pewter light, stretched tightly over the fine bones. And her lips, they'd felt so incredibly soft; even now they were still slightly quivering.

It had been so long. The keen knife-edge of yearning twisted inside him. God, he missed kissing. Missed those sweet, languorous, soul-destroying wet kisses Robyn was so good at. Emma licked her lips and heat surged in his loins. A

sudden urge swept over him to take her into his arms once
more and kiss her. Just to comfort her. *No, not just that*, a
voice inside warned.

He came to himself with a start. What kind of damn fool
was he? He must be losing it!

Comfort was the last thing she wanted from him. He repelled her. No way would she want to go to bed with him,
and just as well. Why was he even thinking about it? *Get it
out of your head, Sam. Get back to business, you moron.*

"Come on, Emma, what do you say? Can you do it?"

"I don't have much choice. I've signed on the dotted line."
Then she turned to look at him and her face was illuminated
by moonlight. Her forlorn expression tugged uncomfortably at his heart. "Good night Mr. Cooper. I'll see you in the
morning."

He turned and watched her go, a slender silhouette against
the lights of the house, and once again he was swamped by
the vivid memory of how she had felt in his arms, all soft,
smooth fragrant skin and lush curves. This was insane. His
stomach muscles clenched with a sick pain as he watched her
go. He couldn't turn away until she had disappeared around
the corner of the house.

The silence descended again; the silence of a country night,
filled with the chirp of crickets and the lapping of the water.

He rubbed at the back of his neck. God, he was tired. Even
more, he was disturbed and dissatisfied with his own behavior. Why had he done it? Why had he kissed her? He knew
damn well that it wasn't just to prove a point. Right from the
start he hadn't been acting normally around her. Right from
the start he had wanted her. It was only sex, but damn it, why
did it have to be her?

Brooding and restless, he slowly headed for the little A-
frame cabin that would be his home for the next six weeks.
Anger, he could understand. And God knows, he'd de-

served that slap. But she hadn't just been angry, she'd been petrified, shaking like a leaf, her eyes wide and dark in her parchment white face.

Just the memory of her face brought a surge of protectiveness that angered him, made him feel trapped. He deliberately allowed the anger to surface, let it knot the muscles in his jaw and clench his hands into fists.

He didn't want to feel any of that stuff for Emma Jordan. He wanted to be left in peace, goddamn it! Peace, to get on with his work. It was the only thing that mattered.

And yet he couldn't help but wonder. Who was this woman? What journey had brought her to this place such a shivering mass of fear? What had happened to her?

But he ruthlessly squashed the urge to find out. Just as he ruthlessly squashed the urge to follow her, take her into his arms and satisfy his aching body.

He wrenched open the cabin door and defiantly slammed it behind him. Whatever her problem, it was *her* business, and as for the other, he wasn't going to think about that, either.

He dragged off his damp bathing suit, kicking it into a corner of the main room, then strode into the small bathroom and grabbed a towel off the rail. Ruthlessly he rubbed himself dry, trying to push down the erection straining to rise against his stomach.

He gritted his teeth, trying to ignore the fire between his legs as he toweled himself dry. He'd come here to write that screenplay and it had to be great. Too many people were waiting for him to fall flat on his face. And a little while ago he almost blew it. He shuddered as the rough towel grazed his aching nipples and tried to ignore the goose bumps rising on his skin. He wasn't going to blow it again. Emma Jordan's problems were none of his business.

But the feel of her lingered, a tangible memory. If he closed his eyes he could smell her elusive, disturbing fragrance, taste her sweet, lush mouth. He tipped his head back and slid one hand down over the quivering muscles of his stomach until he found the throbbing flesh. Closing his fingers tightly around the hard shaft, he squeezed. The pain was ecstasy. With a groan he let his hand slide along the smooth, familiar length.

He opened his eyes and saw his face, flushed and tight, glazed with need, staring back at him from the mirror. He watched himself as the excruciating pleasure built: despised himself, but couldn't help himself as he thought of Emma and came.

EMMA STRUGGLED UP from sleep, drenched in sweat. She pushed the long, damp strands of tangled hair out of her eyes and looked over at the alarm clock. Five-thirty. Her head flopped back on the pillow. Her heart was still racing, her breath coming in fast, anxious gasps.

That dream again, about Larry. But this time when he looked up and smiled it was Sam's face she stared into. Sam's smile that turned into Belial. And then Sam was kissing her, violating her. But the most horrible part was the way she had acted, participating with a lascivious enjoyment that made her feel unclean even recalling it.

There was no point trying to get back to sleep. She might have that dream again. She dragged herself out of bed. Maybe a swim would wash away the aching lethargy that made her feel as if she'd been having sex all night but without any gratification.

Hurriedly slipping into her bathing suit, she headed downstairs and out the back door toward the water. The trees loomed like dark sentinels through the soft gray mist wafting over the point, but above her head the sky was already pale with the dawn.

In barely half a day her whole life had been turned upside down, and last night's telephone conversation with Petra had only made her feel worse. Now that she knew the full extent of how her agent had manipulated Sam Cooper, she felt even more embarrassed by the things she'd said. And none of Petra's arguments about it being "all in her own best interests" made her feel any better.

But that was the least of her worries. If it were just a question of apologizing to the man it would be simple. It was the other thing that had her so worried. All this time she had thought she was okay. That she'd come to terms with everything.

But obviously she was wrong. It had never been her intention to hide from her demons, but the coming of Sam Cooper had forced her to realize that hiding was exactly what she'd been doing.

No matter what she might have believed, clearly the past still had its claws sunk deeply into her. Because it hadn't been the physical threat. Or the shock of seeing her own creation spring to life full-blown before her eyes, in all his horror.

No. What lingered, what truly frightened her was the unnatural way her body responded to him, even while she was engulfed by revulsion.

Working with this man was going to be even harder than she'd feared, but now it was plain that she *had* to do it, for her own sake, and not just because of a legal obligation. She had to prove to herself that she hadn't become some sort of sexual deviant and that Sam Cooper was just a man, not some monster from hell out to get her.

A slight splashing sound made her look up and her breath caught in her throat when she saw Sam wading out of the misty water toward her. The wet, hip-hugging black bathing suit clung to every contour of his body, and the bulge between his legs drew her stricken gaze like a magnet.

Quickly she raised her eyes to his sculpted torso, beaded all over with drops of water clinging to the golden skin of his chest, and even that was dangerous territory. Finally she looked up and met his eyes, keen and probing, and discovered the most dangerous territory of all.

"Good morning." His smile was warm, but a little wary. "Are you an early riser, too?"

"Sometimes." She hardly knew what she said as he continued to walk toward her with a smooth, unhurried stride.

Suddenly he reached out and she flinched, but he was only grasping for the towel slung over a branch of the tree beside her. He shot her a searching look as a small worried frown creased his forehead.

Then his expression cleared. "Enjoy your swim," he said casually, and sauntered away toward his cabin.

Emma let out the breath she'd been holding. So much for the resolutions she had made last night.

IT WAS SEVEN-THIRTY by the clock on the microwave when Emma entered the large kitchen, dressed in loose white shorts and a T-shirt. She was wide-awake, alert, and ready to face Sam Cooper again. Ready to redeem herself. She was perfectly capable of responding normally to the man, in any situation that might arise.

One thing at a time, though. Deal with the morning routine. She plugged in the coffeemaker and opened the kitchen door wide.

The mist had burned off already and the lake sparkled blue in the sunshine. On the porch the hanging baskets of trailing purple lobelia swayed gently in a balmy, fragrant breeze that carried the promise of another hot, sultry day.

Emma took a deep fortifying breath of the sweet morning air. She had thought she was past the stage of falling apart like that, but it seemed she was wrong. Now, however, she had herself under control.

She turned and stepped over to the fridge, took out the glass pitcher of orange juice and a small jug of coffee cream and put them on the table.

As far as Sam Cooper went— Yes, there was something disturbing about the man. But she should remember that he was her guest, and perhaps observing the social niceties would simplify the situation, provide the rules by which they could carry out this collaboration.

A tapping noise made her turn to see Sam standing on the other side of the screen door dressed in light khaki pants and a cotton shirt and with something tucked under his arm. The morning sun glowed behind him, turning his hair into a rich golden halo. His mouth curved in a small, uncertain smile that was reflected in his eyes as he opened the door and stepped in.

Immediately his presence swept over her like a tangible, overpowering wave, making every muscle tense and her heartbeat accelerate. His shirt was open at the neck, revealing a triangle of golden flesh. And even though she knew what the body underneath looked like, there was something even more disturbing about him fully clothed.

"Come on in." She forced a smile, a little impatient with herself. She'd just finished telling herself she could cope. And he hadn't done anything except walk in the door.

"I hope I'm not too early."

"Not at all. Won't you sit down?"

"Thanks." He tossed a black leather portfolio onto the scrubbed pine table and pulled out a chair. "Did you enjoy your swim?"

"Yes, it was very refreshing." She sounded like a damn robot. This was not the way to convince herself that she had it all under control. But she couldn't help it; the man made her intensely uncomfortable.

"I'm pretty excited about getting started. I had to hold myself back, didn't want to arrive too early."

She smiled woodenly, not knowing what to say. "What would you like for breakfast?" *Come on, loosen up.*

"Just toast and coffee will do me fine."

He returned the smile, with a radiance guaranteed to raise a collective sigh from a female movie audience, but in her it provoked a more disquieting response. Forcing her stiff legs to move, she slipped two pieces of bread into the toaster and reached for the coffeepot.

Normally she ate a good breakfast, but this morning she couldn't face a thing. She sank down at the table and gripped her coffee cup for dear life, trying to act charming and pleasant, the way a good hostess should. When she did meet his eyes, they were filled with a puzzled sympathy that unnerved her even more. She didn't want to be the object of anyone's pity.

"I...um...I took a walk as far as the gate after my swim." He took a sip of coffee, clearly uncomfortable and just as clearly trying hard to put her at ease. "You have a beautiful spot here."

"There are many lovely spots in the Kawartha Lakes. I have guidebooks you can look over if you're interested in touring the area."

"Thanks. That would be very nice."

Awkward silence fell. This stilted conversation was taking its toll on him, too, she could tell.

The toast popped with a metallic twang. Emma started, then tried to disguise her jitters by rising from the chair.

"Sit. I'll get it." His deep husky voice had her sinking stiffly back down again. "I told you I don't need to be waited on." As he got to his feet the corner of his mouth curved in a smile of sympathy.

Pity for her nervousness. How could she blame him if he thought she was some kind of weirdo? She must be, if his mere presence could make her feel this threatened, make her own kitchen seem like a foreign place.

Suddenly she realized that her hands were burning. She eased her death grip on the coffee mug and took a fortifying sip.

He put the toast on a plate and looked over at her, still with the hint of a smile. "Do you have any jam?"

"In the fridge." Taking another sip of coffee, Emma realized that she was beginning to feel a little more calm.

She watched Sam open the refrigerator and bend slightly to look in, his movements relaxed and graceful. Maybe she shouldn't be too hard on herself. Last night had been one long series of shocks, culminating in that appalling moment of self-discovery.

She had been convinced that the sexual part of her was dead, and it had been, for the past two years; but there was no denying what she'd felt during that terrifying kiss, no point in trying to pretend that the throbbing heat was anything other than sexual response.

She should have been repelled. Her former self *would* have been repelled. Had she become warped somehow by what she'd discovered that day in Larry's office?

"Found it." Sam emerged from the fridge with a triumphant grin, holding up the jar of blackcurrant jam. He came back to the small table and set it down beside his plate of toast.

The warm male smell of him drifted her way and Emma felt her muscles tensing up again, involuntarily.

Come on. You can do it. She had to get this under control. No matter what had happened in the past, it was over, and she needed to prove to herself that it hadn't left her irrevocably blighted.

But by the time breakfast was finished her nerves felt as tight as a bowstring. Between snatches of awkward, murmured conversation the silence crowded in, and every glance of his blue eyes, every jolt of awareness, gave another twist of the screw. The roomy kitchen seemed smaller and smaller and much too quiet, until it felt as if the walls were pressing in on her.

Emma swallowed a sigh of relief as she finally led him down the hall and into her office.

"Great view." Sam stepped over to the threshold of the open French doors leading out onto the veranda hung with a lush profusion of flowers. To his right, at the front corner of the house, masses of creamy roses covered a wooden trellis screening one corner of the porch. Through the trees the lake sparkled, blue and placid in the early sun.

Down at the small beach Fritz stood thigh-deep in the lake, waving a long stick back and forth under the water, sun glinting off his cropped blond hair and the powerful muscles flexing in his arms.

"What's he doing?"

Emma glanced out for a moment. "He's clearing the weeds."

"So what else does he do apart from clearing weeds and scaring the shit out of people at the gate?"

She shot him a disgusted look. "He does everything around here. He keeps the place in shape for me. I don't know how I'd get on without Fritz. He's my gardener, handyman, plumber—you name it, he does it."

"Bodyguard?"

She stiffened. "I don't need a bodyguard."

"My mistake. Keeper?"

"Is this your idea of a joke, or are you trying to be insulting?"

"Neither. Just making conversation."

A baleful narrowing of her eyes was her only response. How many more times did he need reminding that this woman had no sense of humor.

The silence lengthened, vibrating with her resentment and distrust. Before it began to spook him he'd better break the tension. After all, he was the idiot who had created it.

He turned and cast an eye around the room. "So this is where the very talented Emma Jordan created her masterpiece."

Suspicion lingered in her eyes, but he was surprised to see a pink flush spread along her cheekbones. All this time she'd seemed such a prima donna, but he was beginning to realize that behind the prickly hauteur she was really a very shy woman, and her shyness intrigued him. There was something very fragile about her.

"How did you manage to create a creature like Belial in the midst of all this?"

She shrugged. "How did Oscar Wilde manage to write in prison?"

"You know, I stay awake nights wondering about that myself."

Her deadpan look told him she didn't appreciate his attempt at humor. He gave a small chuckle and rubbed at the back of his neck. *Give up, Sam. The woman already thinks you're a jerk.*

He turned back to the comfortable office. Every window looked out on the water and sunlight poured in on white walls hung with an eclectic collection of prints and paintings. A sofa upholstered in fresh blue-and-white stripes faced the stone fireplace across a pickled-pine coffee table.

"To be honest with you, I was expecting something more in line with Frankenstein's castle."

She smiled with amusement. "Perched on a bleak and desolate point?"

He laughed. "With deadly mantraps for the unwelcome visitor."

Emma gave a little bow. "We aim to please."

Her playfulness encouraged him. The lady had a sense of humor, after all, even if it was ruthlessly buried. Why?

"Then tell me something. . . . Where does it come from, all that darkness?"

Her smile vanished and her face became rigid and closed. "From my imagination, where do you think?"

He couldn't help but be puzzled and intrigued by her quick defensiveness.

Emma stood as if poised for flight by the desk set in front of the large bay window, watching him, her smoky eyes dark with wariness. For some reason he made her uncomfortable, and all his efforts to win her over had fallen on stony ground. He hated to admit it, but it piqued his ego a little. Women didn't usually react to him like that. Emma Jordan unsettled him.

He had to *forget* last night. He couldn't let himself think of her in that way again. And if she ever knew, she'd probably feed him to Fritz. Piece by piece. And he knew which piece she'd start with.

He broke out in a cold sweat. He had to remember the reason he came here. The reason he'd been driving himself for the past year. Work. He had to hang on to that. It had gotten him this far, given him a reason to get up in the morning when there didn't seem to be any point in going on.

He was here for one thing only. The screenplay. And then he could leave Emma Jordan to her demons. Or in this case, one demon. Belial.

He stepped back into the room. "How did you luck out and find this place?"

"I inherited it from my grandparents."

On the point of saying, "Lucky you," he bit his tongue. He had a feeling there was nothing lucky about Emma Jordan, despite her success. An air of tragedy hung about her. Another sharp pang of compassion rose up inside him, but he brushed it aside. "Well, shall we get to work?"

"I'm ready when you are, but I'm not exactly sure how we're going to manage this."

Sam suppressed his impatience. "Now what?"

"I haven't . . ." She hesitated awkwardly. "That is . . ."

The awful truth was beginning to dawn on him. "Be honest, you've never done this before, have you?"

She bit her full, pink lower lip and twisted her hands together more tightly. After a long moment she answered, "No."

Oh, shit. "You lied to me, didn't you?" He tried to stay calm. "You said you knew what you were doing."

"So what? You...you frightened me." Two bright spots of color flamed along the elegant cheekbones. "You were absolutely horrible! You yelled at me, you threatened me, you swore at me—"

"All right, already. I was awful to you, I get the picture."

No matter how crazy she made him, there was something fragile and tragic about her that made him bite down on his impatience.

"Let's just get started." He looked around, then tossed the portfolio onto the coffee table. "Here. Let's sit here."

He sat down on the sofa and unzipped the case, laying out two copies of the treatment, his own thick notebook and a well-thumbed copy of *Belial* bristling with yellow sticky notes.

Emma sank down in the chair at the far end of the table—about as far away from him as she could get without leaving the room.

"Now you can't see anything from there, can you?" He tried not to be sharp, tried to curb his rising impatience. "Come and sit down over here. I won't bite."

Reluctantly she got up and moved over to the far end of the couch, radiating tension from every pore. She crossed one long, slender leg over the other. Even in loose shorts and a T-shirt, she had the kind of timeless beauty that once again made him think of something sculpted for the gods.

But she was no marble statue, with her cloud of silky chestnut curls pulled back into a ponytail, the loose tendrils tumbling onto her pale cheek, and that translucent porcelain skin stretched tight over delicate bones. There was nothing cold and impervious about that soft, vulnerable mouth, or the pain deep down in her smoky eyes.

Sam tore his gaze abruptly away, back to the material spread out on the coffee table, with a fleeting sense of disorientation. He took a deep breath, folded back the stapled cover sheet on the treatment and tapped the first page. "I thought we could start with the character sketches."

Emma picked up the copy in front of her and leafed through the typewritten pages—character sketches, background sketches, story outline—his organization amazed her. She read the first few paragraphs of the outline and had to admit herself impressed. Clear, concise, and capturing the tone of her story perfectly.

She raised her eyebrows and looked at him with new respect. "Did you write this?"

There was more cynicism than warmth in his smile. "Surprised?"

"No, of course not." But her protest was in vain.

"You shouldn't believe everything you read in those trashy magazines."

Heat rose in her cheeks. "I'm sorry, I didn't mean anything by that."

"Yes, you did." The small furrows between his brows deepened as he leveled her with a cynical look. "Just so there's no more confusion, let me fill you in on my background. I received a degree in English from the University of Montana and studied at The Actor's Studio in New York. I also did Shakespeare at Stratford for five years—before I graduated to being a dumb stud."

"I'm sorry," she said quietly.

"Forget it. Let's just get on with it."

That would teach her for stereotyping him, but he was so sure of himself, he certainly made it easy not to feel too guilty.

"Why don't you finish looking over what I have, and then we can talk about it."

She began reading, intensely conscious of his eyes on her, then saw a line that made her self-consciousness vanish.

She shook her head vehemently. "No. You've got it all wrong. You're misinterpreting Belial."

"Where are you?" He leaned close to look over her shoulder at the open pages and his bare arm grazed hers.

All the hairs on her arm stood on end and she edged away a little, glancing up at him surreptitiously as he read from the page. From this close she could see that the ends of his long, curling lashes were tipped with a paler shade of brown and noticed the tiny laugh lines that rayed out from the corners of his impossibly blue eyes.

She wrenched her thoughts back to business. "You see, he doesn't lack a conscience. He's a moral creature."

Sam looked up, pinning her with his brilliant blue stare. "How can you say that? He destroys everyone who cares about him."

She could only hope and pray that her expression didn't give away any of the disturbing feelings churning around inside. "His morality is inverted. It revolves around his needs, needs that the writer imposed on him. When he assumes human form the writer realizes that she feels responsible for him, feels a bond with her creation."

Emma stood, taking the treatment with her, and walked toward the veranda doors. His proximity made her nervous and it was hard to concentrate on what she was saying. "You've made him a creature of random evil and chaos, but he's not. He has a goal—to destroy his creator."

Sam stood and walked toward her, his deep-set eyes brilliant with intensity as they never left her face. "I can't understand why this woman would feel a bond with someone who's out to destroy her."

Her heart was starting to flutter. He was closing in on her again and so was the claustrophobia, the hunted sense of desperation. Why did he have to interrogate her? Why did he have to look at her as if he could see right through her and pull her apart?

"Why does she have to have reasons? She created a story, a character that came to life. It's just fiction, for God's sake!"

"Yes, but even in fiction certain rules apply. You know that as well as I do," Sam insisted. Then he paused and pinned her with a relentless, probing look. "You know what I think?"

"No. And I'm not sure I want to." She hated that look, but she couldn't tear her gaze away.

He stood challenging her, his hands jammed in his pockets. "I think that you're hiding something, and if I'm really going to understand these characters, I'm going to have to figure out what that is."

In less than a second she had pushed past him and stood at the far side of the room, panting slightly. "I'm not hiding anything."

"Come on, Emma. You might think I'm a dumb stud, but I wasn't born yesterday. There's something inside you, eating away at you." His voice softened. "Keeping it bottled up isn't going to help."

Her hands were trembling. "Don't try analyzing me. This isn't California. We don't have to have group therapy to write a script. My personal life is none of your business."

"Maybe not. But your reaction last night wasn't normal. I can understand you being frightened and slapping my face, but it was more than just that, wasn't it?"

"What does last night have to do with this morning and work?"

"In order to work with you I have to understand you—"

"You have no right to go prying into my personal life. You're not to go speculating about me! Do you understand?" Now she was shaking so badly, she could hardly get the words out.

He came toward her in one easy movement. "Hey, you can order me to come up here. You can tell me when to show up and when to leave, but you can't tell me what to think." He put his hands on his hips and his face hardened. "I'll speculate as much as I want to. It's part of my job to figure people out and what makes them tick. If I'm going to be able to play Belial, I have to understand."

"I don't care what you need to do," she choked out. "Just don't try prying into my private affairs."

She turned and fled the room, racing upstairs to the sanctuary of her bedroom where she paced the floor, trying to calm herself.

From her window she saw Sam striding rapidly down toward the water, hands in his pockets. Even from above, she could see the tension in the set of his shoulders.

When he got to the small beach he stooped and picked up a handful of pebbles, then launched them one at a time into the lake with sharp, angry movements. He spun around and glared up at the house. Emma darted to one side of the window, out of sight, and rested her forehead against the cool plaster wall.

He couldn't touch her, couldn't hurt her, as long as she remembered that *she* was in control. Let him pry all he wanted, but there was only one way he would ever find out—if she told him. And nothing on earth could make that happen.

She'd kept her secret bottled up inside for two years, and there it would stay.

5

"EMMA." SAM KNOCKED on the bedroom door, his voice low and troubled. "I'm sorry. I didn't mean to upset you."

Standing at the big bay window, Emma bunched the fine lawn curtain in her hand with a tight, desperate grip, trying to find calm and solace in the constantly moving waters of the lake. Feeling like a hunted thing in her own house.

"Please go away and leave me alone. I need a little time to myself."

"Time is something we have very little of, I'm afraid."

Through the door, his words vibrated with strained patience and she felt her anger surface. He had a lot of nerve! Needlessly complicating the issue in the first place, and then sounding like the long-suffering victim of her self-indulgent moodiness.

"All the more reason to confine yourself to the work." Her voice hardened with resentment. "Stop wasting your precious time trying to figure me out."

"I'm not trying to make life difficult for you, but you can't expect me to work with someone I don't understand. Someone who's a great big question mark." Now low and persuasive, he tempered his words with concern. "It's only natural I want to know you a little better."

She took a deep, shaky breath. Know her better? In barely a day he'd seen through her all too clearly.

"Come on, Emma. You can't hide in there forever. We have a script to write, remember?" Now Sam's tone sharpened with a trace of impatience again.

Down under the trees she could see that the workmen had arrived and were filling in that damned hole, with Fritz keeping a dragon-eyed watch. Just seeing his massive, familiar figure made her feel a little more secure. Fritz would gladly turf Sam Cooper out on his ear if she said the word, and for a moment she was sorely tempted.

But he was right, she couldn't hide in here forever. And it wasn't Sam Cooper she had to fear, but what was inside herself.

That horrible sense of helplessness reminded her too much of the way she'd felt at the very beginning, when she had thought there was nothing left of her to go on with. That life was over.

But she had weathered the devastation and emerged stronger for it. She could face these fears and defeat them, too. Slowly she went over and opened the door.

Sam had been leaning against the doorframe with his arms folded across his chest, but now he straightened, shoved his hands into his pockets and smiled. A smile that was a little too bright. "Atta girl. I knew you could do it."

Emma raised her chin. "Don't patronize me, Mr. Cooper. Let's just get down to work."

AND WORK WAS WHAT they did, for the next three days.

True to his word, Sam arrived at the French doors of the office every morning on the dot of eight. At her suggestion they extended working hours to seven in the evening. Anything to get the script finished that much sooner, because then he would be gone.

And yet, in spite of the difficult start, she found the collaboration surprisingly easy. Sam knew the book inside out. Of course there were more arguments, not only over his interpretation, but over which scenes had to be cut, which drastically changed or reorganized to suit the screen. And yet it was very strange to realize that someone else besides herself was so intimately acquainted with her own creation. Especially when it seemed he was destroying it in front of her eyes.

But despite their clashes his dedication and intelligence impressed her, along with a professional attitude that never wavered all the time they were together. He was trying to put her at ease, and she did appreciate it.

But every now and then she'd glance at Sam and experience a fleeting disorientation at the sense of familiarity. She'd have to remind herself that he wasn't any of the characters he'd played in those films. He was still a virtual stranger to her.

And Sam didn't behave like a movie "star." He didn't flaunt his ego, or maybe it was just under wraps out here, far from his own world. Whatever the reason, he was much less self-absorbed than she thought he would be. Much more real.

To her surprise the work became engrossing and stimulating. She was learning all the time, and often became so immersed that she forgot to feel uncomfortable and threatened. If it weren't for this ridiculous sexual discomfort, she could almost enjoy the time spent working with him.

But that awareness was always there, beneath the surface. Like a nagging toothache, she learned to operate in spite of it, but the feelings never went away, so there was no possibility of relaxing enough around him to truly enjoy his company.

Even now, as he leaned back in the corner of the couch, chewing on a pencil, pondering the continuing battleground of Belial's motivation, she couldn't take her eyes off the way his long, tapered fingers curled around the pencil, the shape of his firm, masculine mouth. The nagging tingle of sensibility sharpened into a keen and pervading lust to feel those fingers curving around her body, to taste that mouth again.

He glanced over and caught her watching him.

With a wild rush of horror, she jumped to her feet. "I'm sorry. Do you mind if we knock off early? It's six-thirty already." She was babbling like a madwoman, but if she didn't get out, get away from here, she would suffocate.

It wasn't Sam's fault. He'd done absolutely nothing to encourage these feelings gnawing away at her, nothing more to make her feel uncomfortable. His behavior had been exemplary.

"Sure, no problem." He shrugged and threw the pencil down on the coffee table. "This is coming along fine. At the rate we're going, we'll be finished well ahead of schedule." And then he smiled, the corners of his mouth curving up in that way she was beginning to know so well, as if he were hoping for her acceptance, for her friendliness.

Something touched her, a brief flicker of tenderness. Where had that come from? She felt vaguely alarmed. How she wished he still treated her the way he had in the pit. She didn't want to be handled like a piece of fragile china. It made her feel guilty, because she had been treating him like a leper.

She left Sam gathering up his papers and headed for the mudroom behind the kitchen. A fine, misting rain had been coming down all afternoon and through the window she could barely see the opposite shore of the gray lake and the shadowy outlines of a couple of houseboats heading for shelter at the locks in town.

Slipping on her old red slicker, she pushed her feet into rubber boots and pulled on a sou'wester.

When she stepped out onto the back porch she found Sam standing against the railing, looking out over the glistening green garden to the misty shape of the old willow against the ruffled water.

The rain hadn't cooled things off much. The air hung thick and sultry, almost tropical, laden with the moist, mingled fragrance of roses, honeysuckle and damp earth.

Emma took a deep breath of the heady scent as her gaze slowly traced over him. There was something so irresistible about his bare, tanned feet on the rain-spotted pine boards, the way the worn blue denim hugged the sinewy length of his muscled legs. His hands were pushed deep into the pockets of his jeans, pulling them taut against narrow hips and tight, rounded buttocks. Her gaze lingered where the top of the railing pressed into the fly front and she felt her knees tremble as a throbbing ache pulsed deep inside.

She quickly raised her eyes to his face, only to find him watching her, with a glittering blue intensity that made the ache even more unbearable. And then he smiled. A neutral, friendly smile. Whatever was going on inside her warped mind and body, he was unaware of it. And thank God for that.

Where had it come from? This hunger, this *lust*. It was shocking, frightening even, to be so intensely aware of her sexuality with a primal urgency she'd never felt before. And not just since the kiss. It had begun in darkness, in the pit, when that electric awareness took her over, like a little current sending flickering tongues of fire along every raw nerve-ending.

As he held her gaze the expression in his eyes sharpened, but his soft voice rippled with amusement. "Where are you going in that colorful getup?"

"For a walk."

"Where are you walking to? You look like you're dressed for the depths of the Amazon."

"Where I'm headed, you might as well be in the Amazon." She found herself responding to his lazy grin and saw something quicken in his expression.

"Sounds intriguing. Can I come along?"

The smile vanished from her face at the unexpected question. All this time, he'd kept so faithfully out of her way.

"Well . . ."

"Oh, please. I won't be a bother. I promise." There was something so wistful in his eyes, so lost and lonely, that her heart contracted with compassion.

"You'll need boots." With an effort she tried to sound brisk and matter-of-fact. "The poison ivy, you know. I might have a pair that'll fit."

Emma turned and headed back to the mudroom. Had she actually agreed to have him come along? That unexpected wave of sympathy for him had snuck up like a thief in the night, momentarily washing away the instinct to keep him at bay.

Sam followed, his eyes on the graceful movements of her body that even the voluminous slicker couldn't hide, feeling bemused by her unexpected agreement.

When he'd turned to find her looking at him earlier, her smoky eyes wide and dark with need and fear, he'd been stunned by the sudden urge to take her in his arms, to shape those beautiful curves with his hands and press her close against him. Desire burned, rousing a hunger that had been dormant for so long.

Over the past three days he'd been able to ignore the tiny warning signs, the temptation to watch her, the way her nearness got under his skin. But now it was impossible to ignore. And for the first time, he had a suspicion that perhaps the feeling was mutual.

Now he knew for sure that her cool reserve was purely defensive. For some reason she deliberately put her emotions on ice and served them up chilled. More than ever, he wanted to know why. Underneath that layer of ice was a woman in turmoil.

But clearly Emma found the attraction unwelcome. How much plainer could she have been about not wanting to be touched by him?

As he stepped into the mudroom behind her she opened an old pine wardrobe and began rummaging through it. She emerged clutching a pair of rubber boots and tossed them toward him. "Try these on for size."

He slipped one on. A little loose, but close enough. "Whose are these?" He pulled on the other boot.

"My husband's."

He looked up sharply, a sudden, unexpected tightness constricting his chest. "I didn't know you were married."

It didn't matter, damn it. It made no difference. In fact, it was better.

"I'm widowed."

The intensity of his relief left him stunned. Stunned at his own callousness. How could he react so selfishly? It was Emma that counted. Now he understood. God knows, he understood her pain.

"I'm sorry."

She tossed him a yellow slicker. "Put this on, too. You'll need it." Her voice had a harsh edge to it, but as she turned away toward the door, he saw her bite down on her trembling lower lip.

It took every ounce of his strength not to take her into his arms right there and then and comfort her. But by the time he had struggled into the musty raincoat and joined her on the porch she seemed to have regained control.

"All set?" Emma glanced at him from under the brim of the sou'wester and wished she hadn't been so impulsive.

What had ever possessed her to tell him? But the words had just come tumbling out of their own accord, and he'd been so willing and ready to offer his sympathy. Like everyone else, he saw her as the grieving widow.

"Ready whenever you are."

How could he smile at her like that, relaxed and casual, when she felt like a bundle of nerves? He acted more at home here than she did. But what else did she want from him? Nothing, she wanted nothing.

"I hope you like to walk." She headed down the back steps to the path and Sam followed. "This is a long trail."

"You mean I might have trouble keeping up?"

At his teasing tone she shot him a quick glance, then kept her eyes fixed on the wet gravel at her feet as they rounded the corner of the house and headed down the road. "No, you seem to be in pretty good shape."

"Why, thank you." He sounded amused and when she looked up she found him smiling, his eyes bright with mischief under the yellow hood of the rain slicker.

"I mean, you swim very well...." She trailed off in confusion.

He laughed. "You mean you've checked out my body."

Heat rushed to her cheeks. "I have not!"

"Oh, c'mon, there's no shame in admitting it. I've checked out yours, too, if it makes you feel any better." His voice had dropped to a quiet, more intimate note.

"It doesn't, and I'd like to change the topic." She bit off the words more sharply than intended, but she felt tense and much too vulnerable.

For a few minutes he said nothing as they walked along the narrow road. Beneath the avenue of trees the rain was only a fine mist, dripping softly from the leaves onto the white froth of Queen Anne's lace and masses of purple phlox growing along the roadside.

Finally Sam broke the silence. "What would you like to talk about, then?"

"Do we have to talk? Can't we just enjoy the peace and quiet?"

He shrugged. "Sure, if that's what you want."

He'd prized a crack in that armor she wore and he wasn't going to jeopardize his gains by pushing too hard.

In a few more minutes they were nearing the massive gates where the wooded peninsula joined the mainland. But Emma abruptly veered off the road onto a pathway he hadn't noticed before. A narrow track that led to a smaller gate, set in the wrought-iron fence, right behind the white cottage from which Fritz had emerged that first evening.

As they passed Sam noticed a wooden plaque hanging by the door of the cottage with F. Lang burned into the wood in rounded script.

"Lang?" He grinned. "His name is Fritz Lang?"

She shot him a withering look of disdain at his low humor. "No relation to the director."

"Oh, you know who he is?"

"Even up here, Mr. Cooper, we get television." Her eyes flashed amber and her tone was cutting. "I've seen *Metropolis*, both versions. We might be buried in the country, but we're not complete hicks."

He had to smile. This woman was pricklier than a desert cactus. "I'm sorry, I meant no offense."

"Well, then, I'd hate to think how offensive you could be if you did mean it. On second thought, I *do* know how offensive you can be."

"Ouch!" He winced. "Have you never heard the phrase, Forgive and forget?"

At that moment Fritz emerged from the cottage, stooping a little in the doorway. "You're not going far, are you?" The gruff question was more a command.

"Just up to the quarry," Emma replied equably.

"Well, don't be too long, the radio said there's heavy rain on the way." The advice was for Emma, but he sent a ferocious glower in Sam's direction.

"Don't worry. I'll be fine."

At Emma's husky reassurance Fritz turned to her with concern, releasing him from the disgusted look. After a moment the giant grunted and turned to go back into his cottage.

Sam shook his head. "That guy doesn't like me. I can't say I blame him much. We got off to a very bad start. I acted like an idiot."

Emma turned and looked at him. Her eyes were mesmerizing and dark as melted chocolate. He could lose himself so easily. *Hold on, that's exactly what you're not going to do, pal.*

"Don't take it personally," Emma said quietly, her expression guarded again as she led him through the open gate. "It's just his way. He's very sweet, really."

"I'll take your word for it." So far, Fritz had proved about as sweet as a junkyard dog, and as fiercely territorial. "Has he been with you for a long time?"

"Ten years."

He nodded. "Well, that explains it."

"Explains what?"

"He acts like *he's* the boss."

Emma smiled. "He is very protective of me."

"Why shouldn't he be? You've given him a place to hide away."

"You just don't understand." Her voice got husky and she cleared her throat. When she spoke again she sounded harder. "It's been very difficult for him since the accident. And people can be very cruel. They stare and make him feel like a freak."

He rubbed a hand across the short bristling hairs on his damp nape, feeling like something that belonged under a rock. "I have to admit I did the same thing, and I'm not proud of myself."

At this admission Emma visibly dropped her guard a little, betraying the first sign of curiosity he'd seen in her. It encouraged him to probe a little further. "So I can understand why Fritz needs to hide himself away, but why do you?"

"I'm not hiding myself away," she lashed out, quick and defensive, her eyes guarded again as she turned abruptly and began walking. "I like my privacy, that's all. Is there anything wrong with that?"

"Not in the ordinary way, no." Sam fought down his frustration and reminded himself that he'd made some progress today. "But I can't help feeling that there's more to it than just that."

"Well, there isn't, and now I wish we'd drop the subject."

He sighed in resignation. "If we keep dropping all these subjects, pretty soon there'll be nothing left to talk about."

"That suits me just fine." She strode on ahead, the wet red slicker flapping angrily in her wake, a vivid flare of color against the green trees.

Out in the open, the rain was coming down heavier, though still little more than a fine drizzle. He thought they were heading for the road that he'd taken in from town, but just before the junction she turned off onto a narrow path that led off in the same direction through the bush, straight as a die.

"Does this trail run parallel to the road as far as town?"

"Yes, it does. It used to be a railway line that ran all the way up to Haliburton. They tore up the tracks and now it's used by hikers in the summer and snowmobilers and skiers in the winter."

She sounded like she was reciting a tourist brochure. Conversation would obviously be tough going. And if her tone of voice didn't tell him that she wasn't in the mood to talk, her strenuous pace did.

After half an hour he thought they must be getting close to town. Through the birches and sumachs he caught glimpses of neatly-kept cottages side by side along the waterfront, and the manicured lawns of larger homes.

But at the next junction Emma turned off the trail, away from the lake, and crossed over the road, skirting an abandoned gravel pit covered with scrubby growth to follow a much rougher path that went steeply uphill.

The track leveled out, then followed an even steeper rocky slope up to the wooded crest of the hill. Emma headed into the trees, following a path only she could see.

The green darkness closed in, so still and quiet he could hear himself breathing. Off to his left he noticed the ground fall away and peered through the tangle of trees to see a bowl-shaped depression about fifteen feet across and sunk at least that deep into the earth, like some ancient excavation, shady and secret.

He didn't know why, but the sight made him shiver. There was something ancient and timeless about this place, the shining leaves dripping with rain. Something old and waiting. He had a sudden image of a prince hacking his way through the thorns to rescue Sleeping Beauty in her cobwebbed castle.

Whoa, what was happening to him? Was he turning into Hans Christian Andersen, or something? Ever since he'd come up here he'd been letting his imagination run away from him, and now this place, the feeling it gave him . . .

The sense of foreboding rose up in him again. Was this place waiting for *him*? Waiting to swallow him up and save Emma Jordan from a fate worse than death?

"Watch out for the poison ivy."

Her words snapped him out of it with a jerk. Emma pointed down and he saw beneath their feet a thick green carpet of the low-growing plant.

"What is this thing?" He pointed to the hollow. "Is it natural?"

"Nobody knows. Could have been natives, could have been settlers, but I think somebody went to an awful lot of trouble to dig them out. This hill is the highest point around here, and if I wanted to keep an eye on my neighbors I'd choose this spot." As she spoke they passed another depression even deeper than the first, with mature spruce growing up the sides.

Suddenly they emerged on the very edge of the hill overlooking the quarry, and he tried to shake off the disturbing sense of foreboding. Now he could see a narrow trodden path and followed Emma along it, deliberately walking as close to the edge as he could get. He'd always believed in making his own destiny, but right now he had to wonder if he was deliberately tempting fate.

The trail led into a dense grove of cedars. He pushed in after her, ducking through the branches, and found himself in a small clearing, miraculously free of poison ivy and covered with a soft brown blanket of fallen cedar sprays.

The land spread out far below, with few signs of the small town lying hidden beneath a misty canopy of gray green trees. Only the water tower could be seen, and beyond that the pewter lake fading into the low misty clouds that seemed to hang right above their heads.

Emma pulled off the sou'wester, unzipped the slicker and wiped the back of her hand across her sweating brow, then sank down on her haunches in the clearing, breathing hard from the climb. Through the evergreen fronds she let her gaze drift slowly along the horizon, then closed her eyes, inhaling the fresh, sharp cedar scent.

She opened them to find Sam sitting beside her, looking at her, with something so deep and probing in his expression that she had to look away.

"How long has it been?" he asked quietly.

"Two years." She turned back to face him, her gaze steady. "And I'm all right."

"That wouldn't, by any chance, be when you started working on *Belial*, would it?"

"Yes." Tension stiffened her limbs. "Why do you ask?"

"Well, that explains it."

"What does it explain?" She turned her gaze away to the hazy distance, willing herself not to feel threatened.

"It was probably a catharsis, pouring out all that grief and pain—"

"It was nothing of the sort." She cut him off anxiously. She didn't want to hear another word. "I had a lot of time on my hands. I had to do something."

"Oh, so you just sat down and wrote a bestselling novel." The corner of his mouth lifted in a skeptical quirk.

"I didn't know it was going to be a bestseller."

"You didn't even know it was going to be a book, did you?"

His clear, brilliant eyes pinned her remorselessly, making her feel ridiculously defensive.

"Of course I did."

"So out of the blue you just decided to write a book, like it's something anybody can do."

"Not out of the blue. I was a writer. I have a degree in journalism. I married straight out of university, but I worked freelance and it was always in the back of my mind that I wanted to write a book some day."

"But was it in the back of your mind to write *that* book?"

"I don't know what you're getting at, but I don't want to talk about it anymore." He was too keen. She couldn't stand this prying into her personal motivations for another second.

"You know exactly what I'm getting at, but I won't intrude any further." He stood and walked closer to the edge, looking down where the gravelly scree crumbled sharply away.

"Hell, I know all about intrusion. When you can't even walk down the street without being molested and the public think they own you, everything you do, everything you say...."

"Please, spare me this litany of grievances."

She didn't want to know anything more about him. She didn't want to feel for him. That's what had led to him being here with her in the first place. And this little excursion was turning out to be a big mistake.

He turned and gave her a long look that swiftly went from sympathy to cynical boredom. "Okay, lady, you've convinced me. You're hard as nails."

His sarcasm stung her into wanting to explain, and she despised herself for the impulse. "I just don't want you thinking of me as some tragic, devastated wretch."

The questions were bound to come. She could handle them. She could keep a lid on everything else.

He gave her a twisted smile as his gaze probed deeper. "It would make a great movie."

She returned the smile. *Stay cool, stay detached.* "I doubt it, the details are boring."

"Emma, stop it," he muttered impatiently, and his brow creased in a frown. "You haven't dealt with this thing at all, have you?"

"Mind your own business." She rose to her feet, trembling with the urge to run.

"Look, I know all about losing someone you love." He watched Emma as she stood under the dripping trees, clutching at the yellow hat in her hand, refusing to meet his eyes. "I know all about the pain. I know all about the feeling of desertion. I know about the anger. You haven't really come to terms with any of that, have you?"

She turned away from him. "Oh, please—" her voice dripped scorn and boredom "—spare me the psychoanalysis...."

He reached for her arm and made her face him again. "Don't do this to yourself. And don't push me away. I'm not trying to hurt you, I'm trying to help. I've been there. I know how you feel."

"No. You don't know how I feel. You don't know anything about me!"

He pulled her closer, his body almost touching hers, until she felt that enervating heat wash through her limbs, felt the frightening impulse to give in to it.

"Then tell me," he said, his voice quiet and husky. "I want to know. I want to help."

"I don't want your help. I don't want anything from you, except to be left alone." She could hear the desperation making her voice shake, as if her life depended on getting away from him.

"I can't do that."

Something in his face changed; the clear blue eyes darkened as he probed her expression. And she knew what he was seeing, what he was feeling in her trembling body now pressed against his. *He knew.*

"God, Emma, I wish for my sake I could." His eyes burned into her so that she couldn't tear her gaze away.

Still and waiting, hardly daring to breathe, she was acutely aware of his hard chest pressing the softness of her breasts, his skin burning against hers through the thin, damp clothing. Every muscle clenched in anticipation.

"I wish I could," came his anguished whisper, and then his lips touched hers.

At first she simply allowed the contact, the tingling cascade of sensation. But he immediately opened his mouth on hers, trying to coax a response. Slowly and trembling, her lips parted and molded to his.

She must have moved closer because now his arms were wrapped tightly around her, his hand cradling the back of her head, making it impossible for her to turn away when his tongue slipped into her mouth, warm and devastating. And then she didn't want to turn away. She strained harder against him and raised her hands to cling to his shoulders as a deep shuddery sigh escaped her and she opened her mouth wider, wanting more.

Slow and intense, the kiss continued until every part of her throbbed with need. Rubbed against his chest, she felt her nipples hardening, wanting to be touched, aching to be touched. Twisting herself closer to him, she moaned into his mouth.

"Yes." His ragged, breathless whisper against her lips was a potent aphrodisiac sending a river of fire down every vein. One hand came between them and he cupped her breast, molding it with a restrained touch.

The shock of it pulled her back from the brink. With a superhuman effort, she drew abruptly away and held him at arm's length to keep him from pulling her close again. For a moment she could only stare at him and struggle to bring her breathing under control.

Sam was doing much better. His face was flushed and she could see that he, too, was striving for composure. But it was also clear that he wanted to continue what they had started.

"Emma," he began, huskily and coaxingly.

"No!" She fought the seductive effect his voice had on her. "I must be crazy. We both must be crazy. We don't even know each other."

"How can you say that? Have you forgotten the pit?"

She wrapped her arms tightly around her body, trying to calm the raging need inside—so foreign, so terrifying, so exciting.

"You can joke about it all you want, but I'm not the kind of woman who goes about making a habit of this sort of thing."

But what kind of woman had she become, powerless to resist a sexual impulse? The kind of woman who could be aroused even while her mind revolted?

"Hell, this is all new to me, too."

She gave a humorless laugh. "Now why do I find that so hard to believe?"

"What do you mean?"

"Oh, come on, Mr. Cooper, please don't insult my intelligence. Aren't casual affairs almost *de rigueur* for people like you?"

His expression hardened and his voice became ominously quiet. "When you say things like that, it's hard to believe that you are intelligent, Emma."

She felt her face flame. "I'm sorry, you're right. I don't know enough about you to make such a blanket judgment. But there have been so many stories written about you, I figure some of them have to be true."

"Well, you figure wrong." Now he expelled his breath on a long hiss, raked his fingers through his damp brown hair, then put his hands on his hips. "Emma, we have to talk."

"I thought we were talking."

"We need to talk about what's really going on here," he said tightly, and reached out to touch her cheek, but she stepped away from his hand. "It's obvious that you and I are attracted to each other."

"What!" she gasped, and began to shake her head.

"Come on, Emma, there's too much at stake here to kid ourselves about it. If we do, it could become a real problem."

"I don't have a problem, because I don't feel a physical attraction." Her voice was high and breathless, unconvincing as she stared at him, her whole body poised for flight.

"Don't lie to me. This attraction is very real and could be very dangerous. It could blow everything I've worked so hard for."

"You've got nothing to worry about." She was ashamed that her rampant lust was so obvious to him.

"Yes, I do." He took a step toward her, aggression in every line of his hard body, but made no move to touch her. Even so, she still felt threatened, hemmed in. "The only way we can fight this is by bringing it out into the open where it can't do either of us any harm, where it's so much easier to ignore."

"Let's start by ignoring this conversation."

"Pretending it's not happening isn't going to make it go away."

"Who's pretending?"

"What's your problem, Emma? Why can't you admit what you feel? It's just sex. That's all it is. And you don't screw up your life for sex."

He turned away and looked off through the trees into the cloudy gray distance. And then, as if he were talking to himself, his voice became quiet and sad. "Now love, that's something different. You die for love, if you have to."

6

"YOU MAKE IT SOUND so simple," Emma said, unable to tear her gaze away from his averted face, from the droplets of misty rain clinging to his soft brown hair.

"Why does it have to be complicated?" Sam turned and faced her. Was it only the shade of the cedar grove, or did she see something dark and turbulent in his eyes?

A small wild laugh escaped her. "Aren't these—" she waved her hand as if the action would help her find the right word "—these things by their very nature complicated?" She was beginning to feel the keen edge of hysteria creep in.

"Look, whatever our reasons, we both agree that this attraction isn't smart. Neither of us want it, so what could make more sense than us joining together to fight it?" He sounded so logical, as if he were talking about something prosaic, not this soul-destroying lust.

The patter of rain on the trees was getting louder, and heavy drops were beginning to penetrate the thick umbrella of cedars above their heads and make dark patches on the ground.

Emma shook off the water from her hat and pulled it back onto her head. "We should be starting back."

But Sam just kept looking at her steadily. "Emma, it would be easier to fight this thing if we could behave more normally with each other."

"And what exactly would that involve?" she asked warily.

"To begin with, let's stop avoiding each other, let's try to find a comfort zone instead. If we spent some time together maybe we'd become immune to this attraction."

"Familiarity breeds contempt, you mean?"

"Contempt? I hope not, but maybe we could be comfortable around each other and those other feelings would eventually just fade."

She raised her eyebrows. "Do you think maybe *you're* being a little naive now?"

"I don't know. *We* won't know until we try." The lines bracketing his mouth deepened and he stared at her, intent and serious.

Instinct warned her against committing herself to something so potentially disastrous. She hesitated.

Sam sighed impatiently. "Look, we're both on the same side, right?"

"Are we?" But he did have a point, she admitted reluctantly. Already, just bringing the problem out in the open had given her one less thing to worry about.

"I don't know about you, but I have too much to lose by letting this go any further." His face hardened. "I've worked damn hard and invested too much in this project to watch it go down the drain simply because I couldn't keep my fly zipped."

"Yeah, I get the picture." Did she ever. Much too vivid a picture. But at the same time she felt a measure of relief. Maybe he knew what he was talking about, maybe this thing could be licked.

Finally she nodded her agreement. "Okay, but I have to do this at my own pace. I can't be pushed."

"That's fair enough. As long as you remember we're on the same side. God knows, I'm not looking for any emotional involvement." His mouth twisted with the words and once again she thought she saw pain and confusion in his face, but it was so dark now under the trees that his expression was almost impossible to make out.

The light pattering had become a heavy drumming on the canopy of leaves above. "We really should be getting back. That storm Fritz warned us about is heading this way."

Emma nodded toward the lake. Massive black clouds billowed on the horizon and were scudding rapidly across the sky, pushing curtains of rain across the steel gray water. The light had an eerie greenish hue that made her skin prickle with foreboding and all at once a sudden, vicious zigzag of lightning divided the sky.

Sam pulled up his hood and followed her as she led the way out along the narrow path edging the quarry cliff.

It was just a summer storm, almost inevitable given the long spell of hot, muggy weather. But it made her anxious to get back home, away from this isolated bower so perilously close to the sky. And she knew that it wasn't so much a rational fear of being struck by lightning, as the fear of something just as elemental—the simmering electricity that she couldn't escape by simply running away.

She plunged through the undergrowth toward the trail, Sam close on her heels. He was right about spending more time together. If she was ever going to be normal again, she had to try. But how to begin? How could she learn to behave naturally with a man who made her feel so uncomfortable? Who made every inch of her body sing with awareness?

Even now her lips were still tingling, full and swollen from that devastating kiss. She could still feel the invasive heat, the plunging ravishment of his tongue on the sensitive inner flesh of her mouth that caused a painful stirring deep inside, leaving her throbbing and unfulfilled. Need, desire, whatever name she gave it didn't change the fact that what he provoked in her was lust in its most carnal form, shocking and unrelenting.

The rain rushed down hard and straight, a pelting torrent obliterating everything around them, until the world was reduced to the pounding roar of rushing water and the sound of their panting breaths as they slid and stumbled down the now treacherous hillside.

Suddenly another livid flash of lightning flared and the air exploded around them in a massive crash of thunder. She flinched and reached for him, but at the same moment Sam lost his footing, and began to slide toward the precipice.

"Hey, where are you going?" She reached out and pulled him back just in time.

He grabbed at her to steady himself and then she was clinging to him and his arms were around her, holding her close.

Rivulets of water coursed between the slippery rocks at their feet, threatening to wash them both downhill, but she barely noticed. All she was conscious of was Sam holding her, smiling into her eyes with a warm sensuality that sent the blood rushing through her veins in the same thunderous, pounding rhythm as the rain coming down around them.

"Thanks."

"It was nothing." For an eternity, it seemed, she stood there in his arms, staring transfixed into his blue eyes as she watched them change from warm and smiling to dark and wanting.

He pulled her a little closer with restrained power and she yielded to him, ashamed but excited by the promise of the frightening ecstasy that she knew waited for her, a mere kiss away.

"Sam," she said breathlessly. "We're supposed to be fighting this."

Then his grip relaxed. The smile changed to a tired cynicism and he stepped back, but kept a supporting hold on her.

"The problem, you see, is that you're so damn beautiful and sexy. Why couldn't you have been the ugly old crone I expected?"

"Oh, sure, now it's all my fault."

Her dry tone broke the tension by making him grin and wiping the darkness from his expression, but it was only a tenuous shield for the confusion inside her.

Still holding on to her arm, he continued making their cautious way down the slope. By the time they reached the bottom Emma could feel the sweat running down her spine and pouring off her brow. She felt hot and sticky and filled with the torrid ache of frustration.

Letting go of Sam, she led him across the road to the trail that would take them home. She was mad; she'd lost her reason at a mere touch from this man and she felt ashamed of herself. Who was she? What had happened to her? Where had this carnal creature been hiding all these years?

With heads bent against the deluge, they slogged along the trail, Emma in a shroud of worry. What if she couldn't fight this thing?

Suddenly Sam's laughter rang out, cutting through her anxious abstraction. She turned to find him with his head thrown back, the rain drenching the smooth lines of his face as he opened his mouth to catch the drops. His eyes were closed, the dark lashes wet and spiky against his cheekbones.

Slowly he began to turn, his arms extended, and joyful, warming laughter erupted from him as the rain washed his face, coursing down the strong column of his throat. She was suddenly overcome with the urge to press her lips against the flesh there, drink from the rivulets of water that caressed him. She licked her lips. She could almost feel the hot roughness of his skin on her mouth, almost taste him. Damn, would she ever forget the taste of him?

Suddenly he straightened his head and looked into her eyes. His hood had fallen back, the rain had plastered the hair to his head, and his smile warmed as he looked at her, making her breath catch in her throat.

"I must be crazy, but this is great."

She must be even crazier, but she found herself smiling back. "I know what you mean."

He unzipped his raincoat. "This thing is far too hot." Immediately the front of him was soaked, the shirt transparent and clinging to the contours of his chest. "Ah . . . that's better."

He began walking again, but continued to glance at her with a grin that got wider each time he looked at her until she found herself grinning back at him like a crazy fool.

Another burst of laughter erupted. "I don't remember the last time I went for a walk in the rain. Thanks for bringing me along."

He was enjoying himself, really enjoying himself! In spite of the pelting rain, the water trickling into her boots and soaking her feet, in spite of feeling unbearably sweaty under the rubberized raincoat, Emma was suddenly filled with a burst of pure, unexpected joy.

"You know, it's been a while since I walked in the rain, too." She joined in his laughter and tore off her hat.

If her action surprised her, it surprised Sam even more. He stopped for a moment to look at her with startled alertness, then he smiled and reached out to take a soaking strand of hair and tuck it behind her ear.

"That's better. It's nice to see you smile. It's wonderful to see you laugh."

His comment made the smile start to fade, but he placed his fingers at the corners of her mouth and gently pushed them upward.

"Oh, no, you don't." She couldn't miss the more serious note beneath the teasing. "Now that I've got you smiling, I'm not going to let you quit so easily."

She couldn't help it. She smiled back. She liked Sam Cooper. Too bad she didn't trust herself. Still, she wasn't going to let that spoil this moment of blissful lunacy. She'd been down for so long, she deserved some fun. That this feeling should overtake her with Sam, of all people, had her filled with wonderment.

Oh, what the heck, she might as well let her hair down all the way. She unzipped the slicker, opening the front to let the blessed coolness of the rain soak her overheated skin.

Suddenly Sam's smile disappeared. His eyes darkened, then his expression became hard and unyielding as he looked away and picked up the pace. In confusion Emma looked down, then gave a gasp of horror. Her T-shirt was soaked through and her breasts were as clearly outlined as if she were naked, the nipples dark and tight and aroused.

From that wonderful explosion of elation, she plummeted into the depths of embarrassment and shame. All the more mortifying because she couldn't suppress the humiliating desire, the fervent wish that he had taken her, then and there, on that rainwashed, stony path.

OVER THE NEXT FOUR DAYS Emma made a sincere effort to be more casual and comfortable around him, but somehow, every time 7:00 p.m. rolled around, she still managed to find something to do that didn't include Sam.

True to his word, he didn't push her, but sometimes she caught the disappointment in his face, that she couldn't do better.

The feelings inside her didn't diminish, either. Just bringing them out in the open hadn't made them go away, although Sam seemed to be coping quite well. Obviously his attraction to her wasn't the acute burning torment that she suffered.

By the fifth day the feelings inside her had built to a fever pitch. It wasn't Sam's fault, but she was frantic to get away from his handsome face and the quiet tolerance in his blue eyes, away from his strong, supple body whose every movement drew her eyes like a magnet.

It had been another hot, sunny day. The storm earlier in the week had dispelled some of the humidity but it hadn't broken the heat wave. If anything, it had sent the mercury higher. By early evening a faint breeze had sprung up, but it gave little relief.

Emma was glad when seven o'clock came around and Sam headed out the veranda doors. She felt restless and desperate to get away from her enclosed little world. Maybe a drive would clear her head.

As she slipped into her car and started it up she glanced in the rearview mirror and saw Sam pause on the steps of the cabin. She put the Acura in gear and began to drive off when something flashed past and suddenly Sam was right in front of the car, holding up his hands to stop her.

She jammed on the brakes so abruptly that the taut seat belt cut into her shoulder as she lurched forward.

In a second he was at her window.

"Are you trying to get yourself killed?"

He gave her teasing smile. "You wouldn't do that to me would you?"

"I've been tempted." Why was it that with just one smile he could make her warm and panicked all at the same time?

"Where are you going?"

"For a drive," she said tightly.

"Can I come?" He cocked his head to one side, blue eyes appealing.

"I don't think so." Grabbing the shift lever, she put a foot on the clutch and started to put the car in gear again.

"No, wait." He reached in to stop her with a hand on her bare arm. Her skin burned at the innocuous touch. "I promise, I'll be on my best behavior."

"Is that supposed to reassure me?"

"Come on, Emma, have a heart." He gave her a keen, coaxing look. "I could do with a break from here, from work."

He was conning her now, but she wasn't born yesterday. "You could use your car." She nodded toward the Cherokee parked by the garage.

He shook his head. "I don't know my way around. I'd get lost."

"I'll lend you a map."

He ignored the tart suggestion and continued to shake his head. "No good. I can't read maps." His sky blue eyes pinned her relentlessly. "C'mon, give me a break. I need a change of scenery."

For her this place was heaven on earth, but even she needed to get away from time to time. For someone like Sam it must be a dull backwater where nothing much happened.

"Well . . ." She sighed reluctantly. "I was hoping to be alone."

The scrutiny became more thoughtful. "Aren't you tired of being alone, Emma?"

She refused to meet those perceptive eyes, and turned to look straight ahead through the windshield. "Obviously not."

He slammed one hand on the open window frame. "Goddamn it, stop it! Stop treating me like this!"

Emma flinched in shock as Sam reeled away in frustration, hands on hips, then turned back to her. "Look. I don't know what you imagine I want to do to you. All I want is some company. Is that so hard for you to understand? That maybe I'm just lonely for some human companionship? Someone to talk to, someone to have some fun with."

His face was tight and hard. "Don't you need any of those things too, Emma? How can you be so damn cold, so self-possessed? He's dead. He's not coming back. Are you trying to die too? Is that what you're doing here?"

Every part of her began to tremble. "How dare you. How dare you bring that up. You have no right to talk to me like this." With a shaking hand she grabbed the shift lever and put the car in gear.

"No, wait." His brow creased with frustration. "Don't go!"

Hitting the accelerator, she began pulling away, turning the car to head down the drive.

One frantic look in her rearview mirror told her that he hadn't given up. He sprinted after her and finally caught up when she slowed down for the first curve. Grabbing a hold of the open passenger-side window he yelled, "Come on, Emma. You have to face up to it sometime!"

"Stay away from me."

She gave it more gas and the car sped up, but before she knew it he had grabbed on to the roof, levered himself up, and his feet were coming through the window frame as he twisted into the seat beside her with stunning agility.

The car lurched to a stop as Emma slammed on the brakes and turned to face him, shaking with anger. "Get out of this car."

"No." He looked infuriatingly calm and obstinate.

"Okay, then I'm leaving." As she turned he grabbed her arm in a hard, almost cruel grip.

"No, you're not."

She struggled, but his fingers tightened, until finally she gave in and slumped back against the seat, her gaze blurring with tears.

"I'm sorry." His voice softened, she could hear his remorse and frustration. "I didn't mean to make you cry. I'm just trying to—"

"Trying to what? Make me feel like a piece of dirt?" She ground her teeth together so hard they hurt.

"No!" He sounded rueful. "Believe it or not, I was just trying to help."

She brushed angrily at her wet eyes. "I don't need your help. And it'll take a lot more than a few thoughtless words from a selfish, insensitive egotist like *you* to make me cry."

"Yeah, you're right. You're very brave," he said cynically, brutally. "Does anything make you cry? That's the trouble, isn't it. You haven't cried yet. You haven't shed a single tear. God forbid you should lose even one inch of that impressive control. Don't worry, you're in control, all right. You're so in control you can't even allow yourself to crack a smile, never mind have fun."

Turned stiffly away from him, she stared out the window at the blurred trees. The worst part was, he was right. There was a movement beside her and she heard the door open. She turned to see him unfolding himself from the seat.

"Sam." She cleared her throat. "Please, don't go."

He stood in the open door and bent down to look in at her, his blue eyes startlingly direct in his tanned face. It took a supreme effort to hold that gaze, but she knew with crazy contradictory certainty that she couldn't look away if she tried.

Blinking away the tears, she licked her dry lips. "Would you like to come for a drive with me?"

His mouth curved in a slow smile that started a mad fluttering in the pit of her stomach. "Thanks for asking."

He folded his lean body back into the seat and closed the door. When his seat belt was fastened, he rested one elbow on the open window and turned to face her. "Where are we going?"

Somehow her mouth formed a tremulous smile and she shrugged her shoulders. "Wherever the wind takes us."

"Sounds good." His grin broadened and there was a warmth in his eyes that told her he understood the effort it cost her and that he was proud of her.

Drawing a deep breath, she put the car in gear once more and put her foot on the gas. Was it possible that, slowly but surely, she was making progress?

Passing the gatehouse she waved to Fritz, who was pushing the old reel mower across the lawn, then turned onto the tree-shaded road that wound its way into town between log homes and white-framed summer cottages. Off to her right, the low sun still shone brightly, striking a million glittering sparks from the choppy lake water.

By the time they went through town and reached the main highway, Emma began to relax into the familiar rhythm of driving. The powerful purr of the engine, the smooth response as she geared up, building speed until they were flying along the blacktop. She slipped a CD into the car stereo, her favorite driving music. Soon the first urgent strains of David Bowie's "Scary Monsters" filled the car and she leaned over to turn it up loud.

The empty black ribbon of highway wound on ahead of them as old farmhouses and shining green fields of corn flashed by. Blue sky above, Sam beside her, she felt a sudden acute pang of happiness and turned to look at him, only to find him watching her. Leaning back at his ease, his elbow hanging out the open window, he rested his cheek against his fist as the wind ruffled through his hair.

And now her simple pleasure was overlaid with something dark and disturbing, then vanished completely as he kept on staring. Every time she glanced away from the road she found his piercing blue eyes on her face. The tension grew inside her until she couldn't take it for another second.

"Please stop that," she begged finally.

"Sorry," he murmured, and shifted in his seat to look ahead.

Passing through the picturesque village of Bobcaygeon, Emma eased off on the gas. Within minutes the town was left behind as she accelerated again, but it wasn't so easy to escape the tense atmosphere in the small car.

And this was only a symptom of the nerve-tingling awareness that kept scraping away at her composure, every single day.

"Look," she said finally, her eyes fixed on the road ahead. "I really don't think this is going to work. Write the screenplay by yourself. I realize now you *are* capable. Besides, I'm busy on my next book. As Petra says, I need to strike while the iron is hot."

"What are you working on, another erotic horror?"

"Sort of. The main character is a reincarnation of the Marquis de Sade."

"Sounds right up your alley." There was an annoying smirk in his dry voice. "I can hardly wait to read it, but right now you're committed to me and I won't let you back out."

She darted a glance and found him looking at her again, his arms folded with infuriating complacency.

"You can't stop me," she protested.

"No, I can't. But if you do back out, you're a coward."

"Only in your opinion."

"Yours, too."

Emma gripped the wheel tighter. Damn the man. Why did he have to be right?

"C'mon," he continued, "where's your ambition? Don't you want to see what we can accomplish?"

"Yes, but I know when to quit."

"You mean because of this thing between us?" he asked bluntly. "What are you worried about? We've had that conversation, remember?"

"Yes, I remember," she said tartly. "Do you?"

"How could I forget?"

She shot him a quick glance. "Then stop staring at me. It's making me very uncomfortable."

Heaving a massive sigh, he turned to look out his window, but not before she caught sight of his mouth curving in an amused, satisfied smile.

BY THE TIME SHE PULLED back in through the gates the sun was dipping below the horizon in a blaze of vermilion cloud and Emma had to admit to herself that she was feeling a lot more comfortable.

Over the past two hours she'd given Sam a whirlwind tour, circumnavigating the nearby countryside, through Fenelon Falls to Bobcaygeon, past the locks at Buckhorn and into Lakefield, where they stopped at Hamblin's parlor for ice cream before heading back home again.

Shutting off the engine, she slipped out and closed her door as Sam did the same.

"See you tomorrow morning." She smiled at him over the roof of the car.

He nodded. "Thanks for taking me along. I had a good time."

"Compared to what, hitting the casinos in Monaco or skiing in Gstaad?"

"They're just places," he said with a small careless shrug.

"Beautiful, exotic, exciting places."

"For me the excitement comes from who I'm with, as much as where I am."

"Oh . . ." She didn't know how to respond to the implied compliment.

"And I find being with you very exciting." His voice was low and intimate, and she tried to suppress the quiver of anticipation that raced through her.

"You're only saying that because it's true." She was careful to keep her voice light and amused.

Sam looked confused for a moment, then began to laugh. "You're full of surprises. I fully expected you to—"

"You fully expected me to get all coy and say you were exaggerating, which of course you were, but politeness demands that you deny it and we would argue back and forth and finally you would win. I would graciously concede and it would then be established that I am an exciting person to be with and we'd both know we were just being polite in the first place," she finished in a rush.

He slowly clapped his hands as a mocking smile curved his lips. "You have it all figured out, don't you?"

"Yeah, I'm a clever girl."

"Too clever for your own good." He shook his head slowly. "What has made you so cynical?"

"What has made you so nosy?" she retorted, trying not to get defensive.

"You."

The one softly spoken word left her with nothing to add. She just stood there feeling vulnerable.

"Now, if I can say this without causing another argument, I *did* have a good time. It was fun. And relaxing. You're a good driver."

"Thanks." All of a sudden she felt absurdly shy at the warm approbation in his smile.

"See you in the morning, Emma." He turned and walked away toward the A-frame.

She watched him go with a feeling close to wistfulness. For the first time in so very long, she didn't feel like being alone. But she brushed the feeling aside and walked into the house.

The orange light of sunset was already fading and the shadows were beginning to gather in the corners. The house seemed so big and empty, so quiet. She walked restlessly through the rooms, turning on lights, putting on some music.

In the living room, she picked up her book from the coffee table, then threw it down again. She didn't feel like reading or watching TV, and after that ice cream she wasn't hungry for dinner.

Her thoughts kept drifting persistently in one direction. Finally she gave in and wandered into the office, to look out through the trees at the small cabin on the shore, at the glow of light in the windows, so welcoming and cozy.

What on earth was she doing? Impatient with herself, she turned and went quickly upstairs.

Ten minutes later she was in her bathing suit, towel in hand, padding barefoot over the mossy ground toward the water in the rapidly failing light.

Skirting the mound of earth where the pit had been, she had to admit that Sam was right. It really did look like a freshly dug grave. Had it only been two weeks since he literally fell into her life?

Two weeks since something inside her had been awakened. Two weeks of painful awareness that just kept building until, right now, every inch of her skin felt unbearably sensitized.

In the hot, velvety darkness, the very air felt as if it were caressing her, like gossamer fingers stroking over her, soft and moist. Straining against the bathing suit, her breasts felt heavy with that tormenting ache that nagged her constantly. The slight friction of the stretchy fabric against painfully erect nipples was almost unbearable. Night and day, her body throbbed in a constant state of arousal and it all had to do with that man in the cabin.

She looked up through the trees to see the three-quarter moon had risen in the sky and a great yearning shuddered through her. What did she want? She wanted Sam.

Are you mad? Are you crazy?

"Great minds think alike, I see."

Every single hair on her nape prickled to attention at the sound of that low, gravelly voice. She jerked around to see him coming toward her dressed in brief black shorts and he, too, held a towel clutched in one hand. His smile was easygoing and confident, the smile of a man used to having what he wanted.

Her breath caught in her throat and she could only stare, her eyes slowly tracing the moonlight gleaming on the smooth, muscled contours of his chest and strong shoulders.

"Oh, hello." She turned abruptly, shying away from eye contact.

Her heart was galloping and she thanked God for the fragrant darkness that would conceal the burning heat in her face.

But in spite of the shyness, excitement gripped her as she boldly continued on into the water. Even twenty-four hours ago, she'd have gone running for the shelter of home. Either she was making progress, or playing with fire. But why not? After all, like the two sensible people they were, they'd already decided that nothing was going to happen.

And she'd never really believed that the attraction he felt for her was anything like the ungovernable impulse she felt toward him.

Emma waded in slowly up to her hips. The cool water felt so good on her hot, sticky, aroused flesh. It might bring her to her senses, douse the fires that raged inside her.

Splashing sounded behind her, then Sam ran past, diving in cleanly to come up a few yards ahead.

He shook the water out of his eyes and the moonlight caught the challenging gleam in his expression. "You coming, or are you one of those wusses who take an hour to get wet?"

He flashed her a wicked, irresistible smile and she couldn't help responding. She found herself wading toward him, dimly aware of the night sounds around her.

His eyes held hers with hypnotic intensity. Then suddenly he lay back and turned in the water, moving away from her with powerful strokes. A chill shuddered through her and she swiftly submerged, trying in vain to quench the confusion swirling around inside. She'd played Trilby to one Svengali. Surely that was enough.

Suddenly he surfaced beside her, his thigh brushing hers underwater and sending a shock through her leg. She swiftly trod water until a few feet separated them. But their faces were level and she stared into his eyes, gleaming in the moonlight.

With his wet hair slicked and droplets of water shining on his skin, the clean strong lines of his face were sculpted in silver light. The firm curve of his jaw, the square brow, the slight irregularity of that broken nose. A man's face, unadorned and beautiful.

"This is great," he said, grinning, his teeth even and white. He had such a nice smile. "And you don't even have to worry about sharks."

"True, but we do have some pretty big muskie in these parts. They hunt at night, you know."

He chuckled, but looked a little uncertain, and when he cast a surreptitious glance at the water around him, Emma began to laugh, once again tingling with heady excitement.

"I assure you it's quite safe. I swim here all the time at night."

"I'll take your word for it. Where I grew up we didn't have water like this. We had a river, a wild mountain river. You wouldn't want to swim in it."

"What else did you have, besides the river?"

"Well, let me see. A thousand acres of the most beautiful mountain scenery. Grizzly bears and bighorn sheep. And cattle and horses. You could ride for days and not see another human being."

"It sounds beautiful. How could you stand leaving it all behind?"

"There have been compensations." Something in the way he looked at her made her feel that she might be one of them. It was a confusing, thrilling feeling. "And I do go back. After Robyn died I couldn't stand being in L.A. It was nice to be able to go home."

It was the first time he'd mentioned his wife's name, the first time he'd really said much that was personal and revealing.

"Are your parents still there?"

"Yep. And my younger brother. Zach helps my dad run the place. I'd like to show it to you sometime."

He talked as if there was a future for them, and it made her feel strange and uneasy. "I can't imagine there being an opportunity."

"Well, you never know. Stranger things have happened. I'd love to show you Montana. It's wild and rugged." He gave her a wicked smile. "You know, the kind of place where men are men—"

"And the sheep are nervous?" she shot back without thinking, then clamped a wet hand over her mouth. What had possessed her?

A sudden deathly silence fell, then Sam threw back his head and roared with laughter. "Emma Jordan—" he shook his head "—I would have never expected something like that out of you."

"I'm sorry. It's just my perverse sense of humor. Larry always said—" She came to an abrupt stop. She wasn't about to spoil the moment by bringing Larry into it.

"What did Larry always say?" Now the smile had vanished from his face and he was looking at her intently.

"Nothing." Abruptly she struck away from him, but not before she heard his frustrated sigh. For a few minutes she swam resolute lengths parallel to the shore, trying to shake off that disturbing feeling.

Finally she lay back on her elbows in the shallows and tipped her head up to look at the stars dotting the velvety blackness of the night sky. From somewhere out in the night came the long, lonely call of the loon, that achingly beautiful sound that always sent a shiver down her spine.

And then she realized that she was listening for something else. For Sam. He'd swum out of sight, and with a sudden quiver of concern she wondered where he was, out there in the darkness in a strange lake.

"Sam." She stood in the shallows and called into the night. There was no answer. "Where are you?" Anxiety made her voice a little sharper as it echoed over the water.

She realized with a small shock that it mattered to her if something happened to him.

Alerted by a faint splash, she caught a flash of movement in the distance and saw him swimming slowly back around the point. He stood when the water was waist-high and began to wade toward her.

"Were you calling me?"

A surge of ridiculous relief flooded through her. "Yes . . . I . . . I didn't know where you were."

"Did you think I'd been eaten by a giant muskie?" he teased.

"Anything is possible." But she didn't smile back.

"Hey, you weren't worried about me, were you?" he murmured as he came closer.

"Well, you are my guest."

He was watching her with that keen penetration she knew so well, as if he knew what was going on in her head, as if he knew how lame and how inaccurate that explanation was.

"I'm here, and I'm safe, Emma." No teasing in his voice now. Just a quiet intensity that stole her breath away.

In the moonlight his wet flesh gleamed, sculpted and perfect, and the shorts clinging to his narrow hips hid little of that perfection. A sudden flush swept over her, until the light breeze raised goose bumps on her heated skin.

"I think maybe it's time for me to go in," she said quietly.

"Not yet. Please don't go yet."

She didn't move, didn't really want to, only turned her head to examine the distant shore. Far across the water occasional moving lights picked out the highway that followed the lake. She heard him come closer, then stop, and finally turned her gaze back to find him beside her.

He gave her a small smile. "I have a place in Malibu—" of course he would "—but it's nothing like this. This is so quiet, so peaceful." His voice grew softer, caressing her in the darkness.

"Yes, there's no place I'd rather be."

"And right now there's no place I'd rather be, either," he said in a husky murmur.

His eyes gleamed in the moonlight, slightly mesmerizing. He raised his hand to push streaming wet hair back from his forehead and smiled at her, the small creases on either side of his mouth drawing her attention to his finely molded lips. They looked wet and firm and suddenly she desperately wanted to feel those lips pressed to hers again.

A violent tremor shuddered through her. There was no denying or ignoring that primitive pull deep inside. Once more, the only option left was escape.

"That's enough for me. Time to call it a night." Trying not to let the desperation show, she turned and began wading out.

"Yeah, I guess it's getting late." But the response was automatic.

He couldn't help watching her, the hunger burning through him as his gaze traced the curve of her slender waist, the sweetly tempting swell of her hips. Just the way she moved aroused him, her long, slim legs flashing gracefully in the moonlight. The clinging fabric of her bathing suit only teased his imagination with fantasies of stripping it away. God knows, he needed no encouragement. His imagination had been running rampant ever since he'd met her. He followed her up to the beach as she moved toward the tree where her towel was slung.

Little did he know when he came here that this woman would prove to be such a lethal distraction. One that he just couldn't afford. Especially now, when he had so much at stake and needed to focus.

"Well, good night." She could feel him watching her, feel his gaze burning into her skin.

"Wait. Don't go. Don't go yet."

Emma found herself hesitating as she turned to face him. "I really should be going in." She tried to hold his gaze, but something quivering inside made that impossible. "I need to get some sleep." Her voice sounded breathless in the humid hush of night.

"Could you? Sleep?"

Her legs began to shake and she was having difficulty breathing. She turned away and grabbed the towel off the willow branch. "I'm going to try."

If only she could control the wild pounding of her racing heart. Her body vibrated, taut and expectant, every nerve focused on the quiet sound of his breathing behind her.

"Emma," he said softly. "This isn't working, is it?"

"Yes, it is. It's working just fine." So why did she sound so desperate?

"It's not working fine for me." And now she could feel the heat of his body so close to her, his warm breath stirring the tendrils of hair curling onto her cheek. "I can't sleep at night for dreaming of you. And during the day, just being near you . . . hurts." Longing grated in his low husky voice.

"No, Sam," she whispered in anguish. "Stay away from me."

"I can't. I just need to touch you. I have to." His warm, damp hands were shaking as they closed on her upper arms.

She shut her eyes in an agony of wanting, frantically fighting the need for fulfillment throbbing deep inside. Giving in would be her downfall.

It took a supreme effort to concentrate enough to get the words out. "You said yourself if we faced it together we could fight this."

"I've tried. We've both tried. But it's not working, is it?"

His hot mouth grazed her jaw and she had to will herself not to turn in his arms. But now his muscled length was pressed against her back and she felt herself weakening, her legs giving way. And that enervating heat was pouring through her like a river in flood.

"Can't we just try a little harder?" she gasped, fighting hopelessly against what she knew must inevitably come.

"We should." He turned her around and she stared, spellbound, into his glittering eyes. "But it's so much easier to just give in," he whispered, as his mouth came down on hers.

7

SHE SHOULD PULL AWAY. She should tear herself out of his arms and not stop running until she reached the house.

But instead she abandoned herself to the hard, desperate hunger of his mouth, clinging to his lips, so wet and firm against hers, sending a raw torrent of sensation washing through her. Aware of nothing but the feel of his body pressed against her, slippery and hard, his hands molding her to him as if he wanted to absorb her into his flesh.

At first she could only clench her fists on his shoulders, but without conscious intention she felt her fingers relax to curve over his warm, supple skin and explore the rippling muscles of his back.

Moans and sighs mingled on the soft night air and she hardly knew which came from her own throat. His hands slid down her back to squeeze her buttocks and pull her tightly to him, and his hard arousal pressed against her stomach.

He pulled away from her mouth a fraction. "Emma you're driving me crazy. How can you not know it? Am I driving you crazy, too?" And then he rained hot kisses down her neck, onto the upper curve of her breast with an anguished whisper, "Please say you want me as much as I want you."

Yes. Yes. And more! She almost gasped the words aloud as his lips closed around her taut, aching nipple through the thin bathing suit fabric. Shocking electric heat singed a path straight down to her feminine core, and she felt herself melting, felt the hot gush of liquid between her thighs.

But just as her head fell back in surrender to the sensation, a picture flashed into her mind, then another, and another, each more ugly and loathsome than the last. *Larry!* The silent scream filled her ears and a wave of suffocating claustrophobia swept over her.

She struggled frantically. "No, Sam. This is a mistake. Let me go."

He resisted for a moment, his hands kneading her breasts, his hot mouth on her nipple, urgently suckling. "Not now Emma," he gasped against her skin.

"Let me go! This is sickening, this is depraved! Do you understand?" She pushed him hard. He reeled backward and she saw the stark lines of his shocked face in the moonlight.

"What are you saying? This is normal . . . between a man and woman attracted to each other—"

"No!" she screamed, then turned and ran.

Reaching the house, she dashed upstairs as if the devil were at her heels, tearing off her bathing suit like a wild woman as she ran into the bathroom. Panting and shaken, she flicked on the overhead light, then flicked it off again, after catching a glimpse of herself in the full-length mirror. She didn't even want to look at her traitorous body. Instead she turned on the small lamp by the tub, then yanked the taps on full.

Clouds of steam began to fill the room as Emma climbed into the bath. She would cleanse herself of every vestige of his touch, the feeling of his hands, his mouth. She would erase every trace of him if she had to scrub her skin raw.

THE HANDLE OF THE BACK door turned easily. Unlocked, as usual. Once inside, Sam stopped and listened, but he couldn't hear a sound. Again the house brooded silently, waiting for him.

Through the dark kitchen and out into the hallway he had only the ticking of the clock for company, and the faint slap of his own bare feet on the oak boards. The entire first floor lay in darkness, except for a small lamp burning on the hall table that gave a feeble light to the lower part of the staircase.

He climbed into the shadows of the second floor, every footstep accompanied by a slight creaking of the stairs, until he reached the wide landing.

This was a big house for one person. Big and lonely. And standing here in the darkness he could almost believe that Emma didn't really live in this house at all, merely passed through it, the way she passed through life, trying not to create any ripples, or let anything touch her.

Light spilled onto the landing from the door standing ajar on his right. But it was still so quiet, and the eerie hush sent a shiver running through his body, despite the sultry heat. He tried to tell himself he shivered because he was soaking wet. He could still feel rivulets of water dripping down between his shoulder blades. But he knew it was the quiet getting under his skin, the protective silence, as if the house had swallowed her up into safekeeping.

Shaking off the crazy feeling of unease, he stepped quietly over to the open door to look in, his feet making no sound on the Persian runner.

Emma's room. He'd spent so many evenings sitting in his cabin, looking up at the light in the bay window. So many evenings with nothing but his thoughts for company.

And the worst of it was, that his thoughts weren't always filled by Robyn and how much he missed her, anymore, but by Emma and what she was doing up here in this big house, in this room, all by herself.

He stood in the doorway, closed his eyes for a moment, and inhaled deeply, filling his senses with her clean, uncomplicated fragrance, the scent of sunshine and flowers and fresh country air.

He stepped across the threshold and looked around the spacious room, divided in half by a graceful archway.

The part in which he stood was a small sitting area. In the light of one small lamp on a corner table he could see more of the inevitable bookshelves running below the bay window, topped by an upholstered window seat. Over in one corner sat a small sofa and in the other a pressed-back rocking chair with a few clothes slung over it.

He stepped through the archway toward the bed, past an old pine dresser and mirrored wardrobe. And then he noticed, lying dead center on the carpet, a damp peach bathing suit.

The sight brought a rush of heat to his groin. He felt frustrated with all her mixed signals, but he knew damn well she was going through a hard time. He had to be patient. But it was almost impossible to remember his good intentions when everything about her was so impossibly seductive.

This bedroom seduced him with dreams of what it could be like for them here, together. Her bed was set against the opposite wall, a simple old iron bedstead painted white. So cool and inviting with its fluffy pillows, crisp white sheets and lacy counterpane.

And suddenly he saw himself lying there with Emma wrapped in his arms, warm and naked against him. Compelled to walk toward the bed, he ran one trembling hand over the cotton-lace spread. His heartbeat quickened, his breathing became a little shaky, as if he really were caressing down the smooth length of her back to her rounded—

A soft sound to his left made him swivel sharply to see a door he hadn't noticed before. The sound came again from the partially open doorway, something between a murmur and a sigh, along with the faint rippling of water.

He stepped over to look in. A bathroom, lit by another small lamp draped with a rose silk scarf that threw a dim halo of warm light, but left the corners disappearing into mysterious shadows. The tub was partially concealed by a heavy antique lace curtain tied back at one side, but he could see a leg drawn up, glistening with water.

Like a man in a dream, he walked slowly toward her, his bare feet silent on the white painted boards, the steamy air filled with the sound of Emma's soft moans. He caught his breath. His heart felt as if it had stopped beating.

He reached the tub and pulled back the curtain a little. Searing heat coursed through his thighs and he was instantly and painfully hard. Emma lay back with her eyes closed, her hair streaming out to frame her face in a riot of damp curls, her lips slightly parted and the bottom lip caught between her teeth as little panting sounds escaped her mouth.

Through the curls of steam rising above the water he saw the very tips of her breasts, tight cinnamon buds just cresting the surface. In the shadowy depths he saw the dark triangle of hair under her hand, saw her hips slowly undulating beneath her fingers.

Her eyes fluttered open, voluptuously glazed and absorbed, and then she focused on him standing above her. With a gasp of shock she surged upright in the water, quickly crossing her arms over her breasts.

"What are you doing here? How did you get in?" she panted.

His gaze slowly traveled up her body to finally meet hers. Even in the dim light she saw the flush along his cheekbones, the heat burning in his eyes. "Your door was unlocked. I walked in."

"Well, you can walk back out again."

"I came to see if you were all right."

"I'm fine. Now leave, please."

For a long moment he only looked at her, and she was suddenly aware of the stillness, the quiet, and how isolated they were in this big old house, and there was nothing in his face to tell her what was going through his head.

With a nod of acquiescence, he turned to leave, but as he reached the door he stopped and turned his head slightly, as if he were listening for something. "No." Then he walked back toward the tub.

"What do you mean, no?" Her throat tightened in panic.

"Not till we've talked."

"We've got nothing to talk about," she ground out.

"How can you say that? What about the way we affect each other?"

"It's nothing that a little self-control won't take care of."

But as he stood looking down at her nakedness, making no attempt to hide the obvious reaction of his body, she began to tremble.

"You mean you can just will yourself to stop wanting?"

"Yes." She raised her chin, trying desperately not to let her gaze stray below his waist.

"Liar." His voice was soft, almost a caress. "You're a liar and a coward because you don't even have the guts to admit the truth. I feel sorry for you, Emma."

"Don't you dare feel sorry for me!"

"I can't help it. You're pathetic."

He might as well have slapped her across the face. The pain, the shame couldn't have been worse. She lashed out. "Just because you're a famous movie star doesn't mean you know all women."

He gave a humorless chuckle, then his voice hardened. "I know you and I'm going to prove it."

He walked slowly to close the short distance between them and her heart started to pound.

"You'll do nothing of the sort. You just get the hell out of here." She tried desperately for the proper tone of anger, but achieved only a breathless gasp. The way he was looking at her right now, it was almost impossible not to give herself over to temptation.

"What's the matter, Emma? Afraid once we start you might never want to stop?" She gasped again and crossed her arms more tightly around her body while he continued. "Afraid I might make you feel good? Alive?"

His gaze never left hers as he sank to his knees beside the tub. He put his hand on her knee and began trailing his fingers up her thigh with exquisite slowness.

She tried to brush his hand away, but to no avail. She was drowning in sensation. She clutched the sides of the tub to prevent herself from slipping under.

"Yeah, well at least celibacy doesn't kill you." She tried to sound insulting, but her breath caught in her throat and she willed herself not to feel the rush of heat, the explosion of need that had her clenching her muscles in the helpless effort to fight the throbbing ache deep inside.

"Is that what's worrying you?" His lips hovered over one hard nipple, his hot breath tantalizing her flesh. "Well, don't worry. I've been a good boy. I saved myself for a long time. Just for you."

"Stop it, Sam." She squirmed, but the movement only brought her aching nipple against his mouth. His lips closed on it with an excruciating explosion of sensation. "Please, don't."

"I thought you could exercise self-control and make it all go away," he murmured against her wet flesh, as his mouth trailed slowly across to her other breast. She arched her back, her hands clinging to the cool, smooth sides of the tub as if to a lifeline. "What's the matter, Emma, does this feel too good to handle?"

His hands slid over her in a teasing dance, skirting one dangerous spot only to brush tantalizingly close to another over agonizingly sensitized skin, until she thought she'd go out of her mind.

"Okay, okay, I admit it. I feel desire, but I'm not an animal without any will or capacity to reason." Her breath came in panting gasps as his hand slid up until it was cupping her breast. Desire and instinct battled between the need to escape and the even more powerful need to give in. "I don't have to act on everything I feel."

"You don't have to. But it feels so good to give in sometimes, don't you think, Emma?" His warm fingers kneaded her breast and he flicked the tip of his tongue across the tightly budded peak. She gasped as her eyes closed in tormented surrender. "Emma, give in to me. I could make you feel so good." His warm breath fanned her lips and she could feel his heat as he whispered, "Better than you've ever felt before, Emma. I could take you to heaven."

"I've had sex before. The farthest I made it was the tenth floor of the Hilton." She tried for a cynical drawl but it came out too shaky.

"Well, it wasn't with me." He gave a deep chuckle, she could feel the vibration against her wet flesh. "When I make love to you, you'll hear angels sing."

"You've been reading your own hype, haven't you?"

"I'll prove it to you."

"No," she moaned, but her back was arching of its own accord and then she felt him draw her nipple into his hot mouth and suckle with almost painful fervor.

At the same time his fingers found her again and penetrated, sliding rhythmically. Her eyes closed as sensation engulfed her. Helplessly she found her hips moving against the urgent pressure, craving more, wanting it harder, faster. The rush of liquid heat was almost suffocating and she could hardly gasp out, "We shouldn't. I can't. Please stop!"

But even as she made her anguished plea the sensations were spiraling out of control, rushing her to the brink. And then suddenly he stilled.

Biting back the urge to gasp *Don't stop!* she opened her eyes and focused on him through a desperate haze of red-hot desire.

He drew his hand away with a small sigh. "Maybe you'll change your mind when you've had time to think," he murmured. "Sleep on it."

What! How dare the son of a bitch actually listen to her this time!

Then he got to his feet. She felt a cool chill where his mouth had been as every frayed nerve in her body screamed for fulfillment. He turned and walked out. She was all alone.

SLEEP WAS PRECISELY what she couldn't do, no matter how hard she tried through the dark hours of the night. At six-thirty the sky was light and she finally stopped fighting it and got up.

Slipping on a T-shirt and shorts, she went downstairs, made a pot of tea and carried her steaming cup out onto the veranda and continued toward the water.

Sinking down onto the rough bark of her favorite perch, the outstretched willow branch, she sipped her tea and looked out over the lake. Mist still hung over the surface, softening the outlines of the trees and graying the colors in the pale light.

It was so utterly peaceful. She loved the early morning, loved all times of day in this beautiful place. Thank God for the tranquillity she had finally found here.

A tranquillity that had been shattered with the arrival of Sam Cooper. And she knew, in her heart of hearts, that she'd never recapture it again.

And as for last night... That drugging sensuality belonged in the realm of sultry moonlight. And now it was morning, and she was alert and ready for anything, including Sam Cooper.

"Good morning."

His soft voice startled her so much that she gasped and almost lost her balance, but he was there, holding her from behind. She could feel the strength in the arm curling around her waist, pulling her back toward his chest. Through the thin fabric of her T-shirt, she could feel the warmth and hardness of his bare skin against her back.

She had automatically clutched his forearm, her fingers closing around the solid muscles to feel them flex beneath her hand. And then a moment later she was free and steadier on her perch, but her heart was beating so hard and fast she could barely breathe.

He swung one long leg up and over, straddling the branch as though he were on a horse, and gave her a lazy smile. "Did you sleep well?"

"Very well. And you?" She deliberately made her answer tart and brusque.

"You're lying to me again, Emma," he said with a smile— that devastating smile. "But that's all right. I can be honest for both of us. No, I didn't sleep a wink. I tossed and turned all night, wanting you. I was in agony."

He was wearing the black bathing trunks again and had a towel draped around his neck. His chest looked golden and smooth, the muscles well defined, his skin gleaming slightly. She wrenched her gaze away to his face.

"Do you want to know what I had to resort to, just to find a little relief?" His smile was slow and sexy and held a wealth of meaning.

"No." She could feel her cheeks getting hot. It was no more than she had been driven to, after he'd so ruthlessly left her

hanging, but never in a million years would she admit it to
him.

"It wasn't enough. I still wanted you."

The intimacy of this conversation was more than she could
take. She looked away toward the lake, but felt his gentle
touch as he trailed a finger along the line of her jaw.

"I fantasized about you. I saw you lying on your bed, naked, all warm and rosy, aroused. Wanting me . . . too proud
to come to me. Did you touch yourself, Emma? Did you finish what I started?"

He picked up her hand and before she knew it he had drawn
her middle finger into his mouth and was sucking gently. The
exquisite tingle went right down to her very core.

"I'm jealous," he murmured, as he took the next finger into
his mouth.

She tore her hand away from him, trembling right down
to her toes. "You have a healthy imagination. I just went to
sleep."

"Coward." But his voice was gentle, his smile provocative.

"Don't start that again." She shifted restlessly on her rough
perch. "Are you going for a swim?"

It wasn't a brilliant question, but it was all she could do to
keep her voice casual and her eyes off his chest and lower. . . .

He nodded, bringing his other leg over, then smiled again,
a gleam of blue through the spiky dark lashes. "How about
you?"

She shook her head, morbidly self-conscious. "Not this
morning. I don't feel like it."

"What do you feel like?" A sultry invitation burned in his
eyes.

Before she knew what was happening, he took the mug out
of her hand and placed it on the broad limb. Then, with a
strong grip around her waist, he lifted her to the ground. For

an infinitesimal moment that seemed to last for eternity, Emma stood facing him, his big hands spanning her waist; then he was leading her toward the water, her hand captured firmly in his.

"No, wait—" She stopped walking, her voice husky and slightly breathless. "I'm not dressed for this, and besides, under the circumstances I don't think it would be a good idea."

"Aw, come on, what would it hurt?"

"No, Sam."

"Come on, don't be such a scaredy-cat."

"I'm not! I just don't feel like swimming this morning."

"Liar." He could feel her halfhearted resistance as she twisted her fingers in his.

"Okay, you want the truth?"

"That would be refreshing." He laughed and led her, step-by-step, closer to the water.

"The truth is, I don't trust you. Not one little bit."

"Ouch! You wound me to the core." He couldn't help smiling, couldn't help teasing her a little more. "Just what do you think I'm going to do?"

She wasn't resisting at all now, he noticed with a surge of satisfaction, and the arch look she gave him only widened the grin on his face.

"I don't know. But I *do* know I'd be a fool to trust you."

"I promise. We'll just swim. I won't—" His words were cut off as a steel vise wrapped around his throat and squeezed.

He automatically clutched at the gigantic arm, trying to loosen the hold it had on him as he struggled to breathe.

"Emma . . ." he choked out, as he gagged and gasped. He was almost off his feet and everything was starting to go red in front of his eyes.

She turned and blanched with horror as she lunged toward him. "Fritz, what are you doing! Put him down!"

Desperately she grabbed at the massive forearm, pulling at the rock-hard muscles in a fruitless effort to pull his hand away from Sam's throat.

"He was trying to hurt you," Fritz said in his slow, guttural voice, not easing up on the choke hold even a fraction.

"No. He wasn't hurting me. We were just fooling around. Please, put him down." She tugged desperately on Fritz's arm, expecting at any moment to see Sam turn blue and stop breathing.

Fritz hesitated a moment, then reluctantly relaxed his grip and lowered his hand. Sam clutched at his throat and swallowed, gasping for breath.

"Are you all right? I'm so sorry about this." The thought of him being hurt made her feel sick.

Sam swiveled his head back and forth, with a hand on his throat. "Yeah, I'm all right, although I may have a little trouble swallowing for the next week or two."

But he could still smile, thank God, and her heart leaped, in spite of herself, at that incorrigible, quirky sense of humor and the disturbing light in his eyes as he looked at her.

"Sam, I'm so sorry. I don't know what to say. Fritz was only trying to protect me. He—"

"You hurt her, I'll kill you."

She gasped, shocked by the venom in Fritz's voice. "Fritz, what's the matter with you? Don't talk like that, you know you don't mean it."

"I do mean it." Fritz wasn't even looking at her, but was glaring at Sam as if he itched to carry out his threat then and there.

Her heart missed a beat as her gaze shifted to Sam. With his superior height and weight Fritz could tear Sam apart and eat him alive, but that thought didn't appear to scare Sam. He returned Fritz's aggressive stare with a calm fearlessness she could only wonder at.

"You don't have to worry about Emma, I'd never hurt her." There was no fear in his voice, either.

Fritz looked unconvinced. "You hurt her, I hurt you."

She was getting more alarmed every second, and not a little annoyed. "Stop it, Fritz. You're being ridiculous. I won't have you behaving like this."

But to her surprise Sam came to his defense. "Hey, go easy on him." Sam's eyes twinkled warmly as he looked at her. "I can't say I blame him. That protective urge has snuck up on me, too."

She gaped, at a loss for words as Sam turned to Fritz and held out his hand with a friendly smile. "No hard feelings?"

Fritz gave him a long, suspicious look, then slowly extended his hand. Emma let out the breath she had been holding. Then Sam's grin broadened and with his other hand he gave Fritz's massive biceps a light tap. "Didn't strain your arm trying to lift me up, did you, big guy?"

Unfortunately Fritz didn't appreciate his sense of humor the way she did. The big man turned and walked away after glowering at Sam for a moment, with suspicion still written all over his face.

Sam watched him go, then turned back to her. "You know, I think he's actually starting to like me. What do you think?"

She stared at him in disbelief for a moment, then began to laugh. "I think you're crazy."

"And *I* think you have a beautiful laugh. It lights up your whole face. You should do it more often." He reached out and traced the line of her bottom lip with a gentle fingertip, and the gesture immediately erased every trace of a smile from her face.

His eyes were very serious as they looked down into hers. His hand moved from her lips to cup her cheek, and the world around them vanished. "I wish I could make you smile more often. What do I need to do to make that happen? I'll do anything. Just tell me."

She felt so terribly confused. Battling this unwanted physical reaction was difficult enough, but God help her, she was beginning to really like and care about him.

"Go take your swim." She firmed her voice, trying to break the spell. "I'm going to get myself another cup of tea."

"Emma . . ." His face tightened with frustration.

"I mean it." She pointed a finger at him. "If you don't, I'll call Fritz back."

He answered her with a small resigned shake of his head, then gave her a lopsided smile before turning away and strolling toward the water.

Grabbing up her mug, Emma hurried back toward the house. What was the matter with her? She'd never behaved like this—even with Larry, her first boyfriend and only lover, the man she'd been madly in love with since the age of sixteen.

How clearly she remembered the strange and beautiful way her body had reacted to his first intimate touch. But it had been nothing like the way she felt last night, the way she'd felt around Sam from the beginning.

Her pace slowed as she climbed the steps to the back veranda. When Sam was near she just felt different. She couldn't define it, couldn't explain it. Couldn't deny it. But there was something in the air when he was around. Something besides the desire that was becoming increasingly difficult to handle.

Was she simply starved for sex? She'd never really believed that she was capable of that kind of physical hunger, although she well knew that sex and love had nothing to do with each other. Larry had taught her that. But she never knew that *she* could desire a man without loving him. Desire. That was all she felt for Sam.

Back in the kitchen, she poured herself another cup from the china teapot sitting on the table and put a carrot muffin into the microwave to heat up.

She heard the screen door squeak as it swung open. Once again it was suddenly hard to breathe. Her heart leaped against her ribs and began to race. Slowly and deliberately, she took a long, soothing sip of tea and willed the crazy pounding to settle down.

Like last night, his shorts clung to him; but unlike last night she could now see every detail of the way the wet fabric outlined the bulge between his thighs. She couldn't turn her fascinated gaze away as he stepped in through the doorway and came closer.

And once again she was overwhelmingly aware of the heat of his hard, lean body so unnervingly close, the subtle smell of his flesh. She wanted to bury her face against the smooth skin of his chest and just breathe it all in.

"Is something wrong, Emma?"

But instead she said tartly, "Yes, you're dripping water all over my kitchen floor." She stepped away from him and turned abruptly to watch the seconds flash by on the microwave's digital display.

The silence lengthened. Ten, then fifteen seconds passed. It felt like eternity. Finally she couldn't stand it any longer and turned to look at him, finding his gaze was still intent on her eyes.

"Look," he said, annoyingly calm and practical. "It's lust, right? Pure and simple. It happens." He shrugged. "The answer is obvious."

She returned his steady gaze. "Not to me."

"Let's just sleep together. It'll probably burn itself out." He didn't even blink, just slipped it out casually, so smooth, so practiced.

Her lips curled in a mocking smile. "Forget it."

"Why not? You want it just as much as I do. Admit it, Emma." His voice remained low, but hard with tension.

"I'll do nothing of the sort. Leave me alone, Sam. You promised."

"Come on, you've got nothing to risk. Not even your secrets," he finished quietly, and Emma felt her stomach convulse.

"I don't know what you're talking about."

"You don't have to confide in me, but don't try to convince me there isn't something eating away at you."

His gaze held her captive. She couldn't look away from those gray blue eyes, so intense and serious, but still with something hard in their depths that sent a shiver trembling through her. He made her feel raw and vulnerable and dangerously exposed.

Suddenly he groaned and took a step toward her. She flinched and backed away. If he touched her she'd be lost.

"For God's sake, Emma, I'm trying to seduce you. I wish you'd just allow yourself to be seduced. Maybe this is okay. Maybe it's nature's way of telling us to get on with life."

"Well, I wish nature would mind its own damn business."

8

FROM THE TOP of the quarry hill Sam looked down through the cedars and saw a lone figure on the trail far below. It was Emma, her dark cloud of hair flying in the light breeze as she strode through the long shadows of the early summer evening.

What was he going to do about Emma Jordan? The question had been haunting him all night and through the day as they worked.

Ever since he'd walked away from her in that tub four days ago, the tension had become excruciating. But after last night he had to wonder—when did he stop just wanting a release from the sexual tension and start needing some kind of emotional participation from Emma? He closed his eyes with an anguished groan. *Last night.*

He opened them again to see the white flash of her T-shirt disappearing behind the trees again. She must be headed into town. If he wanted to catch her, there was no time for the usual route.

Taking a deep breath, he dropped to his haunches, put a hand on the lip of the hill and vaulted over the edge. Keeping his body low, he slid down sideways, his sneakers slipping in the gravelly scree. Halfway down, the slope got even steeper. He began gathering dangerous momentum. Oh, what the hell. Might as well go for it.

He abandoned caution and let out a mighty whoop. "Whoaaa...!" With a long, loud yell he raced headlong downhill, expecting at any moment to go head over heels.

He stumbled to a halt at the bottom, half amazed to find himself still in one piece.

Are you crazy? You're getting too old for this stuff.

But then the next moment he set off at a quick trot along the road, toward the old railway track.

Maybe he really was crazy. All day he'd been sure that Emma had noticed his bitten-off answers and dark mood, but she hadn't confronted him about it, just retreated into the private little world inside her head and slammed the door in his face. And he felt damn resentful.

That was it, wasn't it? He wanted to be part of her world. Used to be that all he wanted was to get the hell out of her world as soon as possible, with a damn good script in his back pocket.

He heard a car behind him and moved well over onto the gravel shoulder as it whizzed by. The weird thing was that the script was coming along beautifully. The first rough draft was already complete and now they were into the polishing and fine-tuning.

He should be happy about that, just like he should be happy that Emma drove herself tirelessly. Instead it hurt, because he knew she wanted to hurry up and get rid of him.

At this rate they'd be done well before the six weeks were up and he almost wished he could think of some reason to slow things down.

He turned down the first side road until he cut through to the trail. Off in the distance he could see the white sparkle of Emma's slender figure dappled in sunlight and shadow, moving away from him. He slowed down to a rapid walk.

She certainly didn't want him around, that was obvious. She might be sexually attracted, but she really didn't give a hoot about him.

If only he could feel that way, too. But he cared, damn it. Her loneliness, her vulnerability touched him as deeply as his own feelings. Her pain had become his pain. He wanted to wrap his arms around her and make all that heartache go away. She filled him with a ferocious protectiveness that was so overwhelming it was scary.

Worst of all was the jealousy tearing him up inside. Larry must have been a hell of a guy to leave her so inconsolable. Obviously Sam Cooper could never measure up. He shoved his hands into his pockets and ground his teeth, muttering every swearword he could think of, but nothing eased his frustration. He hated feeling so inadequate. He'd really lost it now. Jealous of a dead guy!

Never in his wildest dreams had he expected to be blind-sided by his emotions like this. This thing with Emma was some kind of cosmic force, as violent and powerful as a mountain river in flood. Maybe happiness didn't come into it at all. He'd had his chance with Robyn and he'd sincerely believed that that kind of happiness came only once in a life-time, if you were lucky.

Sam stopped dead in his tracks in panic and stared sight-lessly ahead. *Robyn*. He couldn't remember her face!

He screwed his eyes up tight and tried to bring it back, but all he could see was Emma, her smoky eyes, her soft curls. His heart raced frantically and he had to force himself to take deep breaths. And then Robyn smiled and laughed in his memory, her blond hair shining in the California sun.

He let go a shaky sigh and began to walk again. It was okay; this was just another step in the natural process. He hadn't forgotten her. She wasn't gone forever, she was still there, in a corner of his heart, and she always would be. But maybe that meant he really was ready to move on to the rest of his life.

Too bad that the woman who stirred his feelings like this didn't share them. So why was he doggedly pursuing her? Because he couldn't walk out of her life knowing she was still trapped by her grief. God knows, he sure didn't want to think about that moment. It was coming way too fast.

By the time Emma passed through the iron arch that marked the end of the trail he was only a minute or so behind. He walked faster, following her across the lakeside park and past the museum. But she didn't continue up to the main street where the crowds of summer visitors thronged the boutiques and restaurants in the low sun of early evening.

Reaching the river, she stopped by the locks and leaned over the railing, a lone figure. No one touched her, no one penetrated that wall of isolation. Emma wore her loneliness the way other people wore their clothes.

A boat was just pulling in at the lower level, heading up-river into the lake that spread out to the northwest only a few hundred feet away. Emma gazed down at the water far, far below, and there was something so bleak in her expression that it gripped his heart with a cold chill. My God, she'd never... Would she?

He hurried toward her, then slowed down, trying to look casual as he got closer. "Hi. Fancy meeting you here."

She looked up, startled, then smiled. "Sam! Where did you come from?"

She was happy to see him! "I followed you. I was on the quarry hill."

"That explains why I couldn't find you."

"Were you looking for me?"

"Mmm-hmm."

"Why?"

"To see if you wanted to come for a walk, of course. What else?" Even though her words were playful her smile was uncertain.

"Put a bullet in my brain?"

She looked startled. "Why would I want to do that?"

"Last night."

Her self-conscious look told him that it was as fresh in her mind as it was in his.

He'd only come up to the house looking for a light bulb for a burned-out lamp. How had she ended up in his arms? He'd had no intention of even touching her, and yet he'd been so lost in desire, somehow she'd ended up naked to the waist, one pale breast exposed to the moonlight.

"I'm sorry about last night," he said quietly.

"Forget it."

Could he ever forget the panic, when she'd pushed him away with tormented eyes? But worse, could he ever forget her mouth so sweet and yielding, the hunger in her kisses, the frustration and desire in her feverish hands? Damn it, she had wanted him.

"I thought, after what happened, you wouldn't want to spend any more time with me than you had to."

"Sam, about last night, I'd like to explain." She looked away, obviously uncomfortable.

It hurt to know that he made her feel that way, but he admired her guts for bringing up something she would much rather forget. Something he couldn't help remembering only too well.

"You don't have to explain. I understand."

"No. No, you don't." She paused, uncertain how to continue.

After darting him a quick glance, she looked away again, biting her lip.

"It's not that I didn't want you . . ." she continued awkwardly. "It's just that I've never— I'm not comfortable with the idea— I've never been with any other man but my husband. . . ."

"It's all right, Emma, I understand. . . ." Her forlorn smile wrenched his heart and he fought the urge to jump in and save her from discomfort.

"I know I must seem very unsophisticated to you, old-fashioned, even . . . but I can't sleep with a man just because I desire him. There has to be more, I mean, for it to be right."

Pain shot through him. *Do you have to be hit over the head with it? She feels nothing for you. Nada.* But for him the wanting had become a painful driving force. And yet the strongest urge he felt right now was to ease her obvious torment.

"I don't think you're old-fashioned. I think you're wonderful and very sweet. And even though I want you so much that it hurts, I respect your need to do what feels right for you."

"I thought after last night you'd be kinda fed up with me."

"No, Emma. I'd have to be dead to be fed up with you."

"Oh."

A crazy surge of hope rose up inside him at that look in her eyes, as if a shy stranger were looking out at him, afraid to trust a feeling as foreign as joy, or even simple happiness.

"It's very busy along here today." Her voice sounded breathless.

She turned back to the scene at the locks and he allowed her to change the subject. Later. They'd talk later.

"Where are all these people going?" He waved toward the boats lined up waiting on both sides of the lock.

"Why don't you ask them and find out?"

"I'd rather talk to you." He leaned one elbow on the railing and drank in the pleasure of just looking at her.

The breeze wafted curly tendrils of hair off her face and her eyes glowed that wonderful luminous gray. He'd never seen a trace of makeup on that smooth, soft skin. Her beauty was so fresh and natural, she intoxicated him.

"Okay, let me see. If they're going south they'll end up in Lake Ontario, and if they're going north they'll end up in Georgian Bay. The Trent Canal System connects those two bodies of water." Her mouth curved in a mischievous smile that belied the prim schoolmarm explanation.

Her mouth . . . He wanted to lean down right now and feel that softness, feel what it did to him.

"Is there anything else you'd like to know?"

"Yes. Will you sail away with me?" It took every ounce of his acting ability to stay light and playful and keep the teasing smile on his face, when he wanted to get down on his knees and shamelessly beg her to become part of his life.

"Where to?"

That smile. Despite the pain still lingering in the back of her eyes, that smile touched his heart.

"Anywhere you want."

"I'll have to give it some thought."

"The thought of spending time with you in a cozy little boat, the possibilities of all those hot summer days and long summer nights, makes me feel a little light-headed." It was hard to remember this was supposed to be casual banter.

"Then maybe you shouldn't think about it." Her voice was husky, teasing, the sound of it raising goose bumps all over him.

He had to grit his teeth to stop himself from taking her in his arms right there, and pressing her against his agonized flesh. He was going to die from the torment. *Don't think about it, you fool. Think of something else.*

The lock had already swung shut as he leaned both elbows on the railing and watched the dark water gradually rise, bringing with it two powerful Chris-Crafts and a sleek little sailboat. "Have you ever been along the Trent system?"

"Yes. Larry had a boat." The sparkle had gone from her voice.

He turned his head to see pain filling her eyes as she stared sightlessly at the bobbing craft.

He bit back all the easy platitudes, waiting for the stiffening and withdrawal that always seemed to follow every time she let slip one of these glimpses of her grief. "I wish I could make it all go away, all the pain. I'd do anything—"

"Let's not talk about this right now."

"Okay. But if you ever do want to talk, I'm here."

But she just shook her head, seeming to shake off the despair at the same time as she drew herself up from the railing, turning to him with a determined, if not completely honest, smile. "I'd kill for an ice cream. How about it?" She nodded toward the Fenelon Dairy Bar across the street.

He smiled back, suppressing the pang of hurt. After coming so far, she was still shutting him out. He was becoming a real sucker for Emma Jordan. He knew now that he'd do anything to protect her, even if it meant protecting her from himself. So he allowed her to change the subject.

"So long as you don't kill *me*, I'm game."

"You really are a crazy guy, aren't you?"

She gave him a familiar nudge with her elbow and he could swear he saw gratitude in the depths of her warm smile. That was reward enough for him.

"Crazy about you, I think," he couldn't help saying softly.

She stared back at him with anxious wonder, searching his face. "You don't know what you're saying, Sam."

"Don't I just!"

"It's sex, pure and simple. You said so, remember?"

It hurt to hear her confusion. "Is it?"

"What do you mean? What else could it be?"

"Look, Emma, all I know is that right now I want to take you in my arms and kiss away every little doubt. More than anything, I want to convince you that everything will be all right, that you can trust me. I would never hurt you. Never." Even as he spoke he wondered just how far his tangled feelings did go. "I'm absolutely crazy about you."

And then he noticed her eyes shift to look past him, all expression draining from her face. He turned to see an older woman in pink polyester, staring at them intently.

"Mother Strickland. How nice to see you."

Emma's lifeless greeting made him look back at her, and he was shocked to see the pinched white mask of her face. The smile that trembled on her lips didn't reach her eyes as she leaned over to plant a chaste kiss on the proffered cheek of the other woman.

"Emma. It's always good to see you." The permed helmet of yellowy gray hair gave a perfunctory nod. Her faded blue eyes radiated hard, cold disapproval. "You haven't been around lately." She pursed her lips and shifted her gaze to glare at him.

"I'm sorry about that." Emma seemed to rally a little. "I've been meaning to pop by, but I've been sort of busy."

"Yes, I can see that." The older woman turned the glare on him again and Sam almost burst out laughing.

Who was this old battle-ax? She was a walking caricature of a small-town harridan and as easy to read as the newspaper. But what did she mean to Emma, to make her shrivel up in front of his eyes into this grim-faced stranger?

"I hope you haven't forgotten that it's Larry's birthday next month." She cocked her head accusingly. "I've ordered the flowers. You can come and pick me up. I hope it doesn't rain. I hate to think of my poor boy in that awful place."

The light dawned. So this was Larry's mother, Emma's mother-in-law. He looked at the woman with more interest. Poor Emma.

The sharp voice intruded into his thoughts. "Aren't you going to introduce me to your friend?"

The woman made "friend" sound like a four-letter word.

"Oh, I'm sorry." Emma sounded flustered and upset and was doing her damnedest not to show it. "Sam, I'd like you to meet Mrs. Strickland. Mother Strickland, this is Sam Cooper."

She didn't extend her hand, but kept a tight hold on her large white purse. "I'm Emma's mother-in-law. Did you know my son, Mr. Cooper?"

"No, ma'am. I didn't have that pleasure."

"I see." She tightened her lips in obvious disapproval and her shrewd eyes darted between him and Emma. "He was a wonderful man. And a good husband. Emma has never gotten over his death and I'm sure she'll never find any man half as good to take his place."

He couldn't let that pass. "But she's too young to bury herself out there with just Fritz for company."

At this the older woman drew herself up rigidly, her nostrils pinched in indignation. "Ah yes, Fritz. He was devoted to my poor boy. He would have given his life to save Larry. It's the reason he's so loyal to Emma. She couldn't ask for a better protector."

This woman was starting to get on his nerves. "Emma doesn't need protection. What she needs is a helping hand back into life."

A small gasp of distress made him turn to see that Emma had gone even paler, if that was possible.

"I'm sorry, Mother Strickland," she said hurriedly. "I'd like to stay and visit a little longer, but I have to get home. I'm expecting a call from my agent."

"You're still writing those books, then, are you?"

"Yes. Yes, I am."

"I'll never understand why. My poor boy left you very well provided for, Emma." For his benefit she added, "He was a wonderful husband. Gave her everything her heart ever desired. If he knew what Emma was doing now, he'd be shocked. Very shocked indeed."

"I have to do something, Mother Strickland, I can't just sit around twiddling my thumbs."

"You could have chosen something more respectable."

Sam couldn't help jumping in. "On the contrary, Emma's book is highly respected. She's become quite a celebrity. You should be very proud."

"Hmm. And what did you say you did, Mr. Cooper?"

"I didn't, ma'am. I'm an actor."

"I see." She looked him up and down with as much distaste as if he'd just told her he was a two-bit pimp. Once again he had to stifle the urge to laugh. "Well, I won't keep you, Emma. Don't forget, the twenty-fourth. Ten o'clock will suit me just fine."

"I'll be there, Mother Strickland," she said in a subdued voice and once again kissed the proffered cheek.

The older woman had barely turned away when Emma hurried off in the opposite direction, along the riverbank toward the lakeside park, without even looking to see if he was following. With growing concern he strode after her.

That cold-eyed old shrew. There hadn't been a shred of warmth in her attitude toward her son's wife, and certainly none of the support a widow surely deserved. At least, not as far as he could see. Just a jealous woman guarding her son's interests long after there was any need.

It was crystal clear that if "Mother Strickland" had anything to do with it, Emma would go on grieving forever. No other man would ever measure up to Larry. Certainly not *him*.

But it was Emma's behavior that really puzzled him. It was clear that the very sight of the woman upset her, and something told him it wasn't just because of their strained relationship. So what was it? The more he got to know Emma, the more of an enigma she became. But it was no good asking her. She'd just curl up inside herself again and shut him out.

He caught up with her halfway across the park, but let her walk in silence. All the way home she kept up a strenuous pace, her face a stony mask. When they reached the house she would have gone straight up the steps and inside if he hadn't stood in front of her and put out a hand to stop her.

"Don't leave. Talk to me."

She kept her face averted. "There's nothing to talk about."

"Emma. I know how you feel."

She whirled around furiously. "Why don't you just leave me alone! Why don't you *all* just leave me alone. You can't possibly know how I feel. *Nobody* knows how I feel!"

Wrenching her arm out of his grasp, she ran away from him through the trees. He watched her go, a flash of white through the long shadows.

"Don't do this to me, damn you! Don't shut me out!" he yelled after her, but she kept going.

Hurt and anger welled up in him until he thought he would choke. He clenched his fists and punched at the air, then turned and kicked at a nearby tree, exploding with a curse at the pain that shot through his leg. What was the use? It was futile. This whole thing was futile.

When would he get it through his thick head? She didn't want him. She didn't need him. He should just leave her alone. But he couldn't do that any more easily than he could stop breathing.

EMMA RACED HEADLONG until she reached the willow and then clung onto the rough branch, willing herself not to break down. The setting sun twinkled off the water—flashes of violet and tangerine light in her tear-filled eyes. Inky clouds massed above the dark tree line of the horizon, their undersides turning copper in the last dying rays of another day. It would storm again tonight.

Why couldn't she wipe her mind clean and begin again? Why couldn't people let her forget? Why couldn't Mother Strickland stop tormenting her with reminders of what a wonderful man Larry had been?

"First, you go numb." She went still at the sound of Sam's low, quiet voice behind her. "You can't believe what's happened. In some ways you don't even really feel it. It's like the whole world has gone mad, nothing makes sense anymore. Like a bad dream, almost like it's not happening to you."

Emma closed her eyes, fighting back the tears, the surge of fresh pain.

"I don't know, maybe it's nature's way of protecting you from the horror of it all." She heard him take a deep breath, and his voice got a little harder. "Then you get angry. You feel like..." He moved to stand beside her now. She could see his hands, his powerful fingers curled around the rough, broken bark, clenching and unclenching.

"You want to... you want to... I don't know, kill somebody...." He ground out the words with difficulty, as if he didn't know how to express what was welling up from deep inside. Yes, she knew that feeling.

"You find yourself looking for someone to blame. Damn it, someone has to take responsibility for the f—" He took a deep breath. "For the mess you're in." His voice dropped again, as if in defeat, and he shook his head. "You find yourself asking, how could she do this to me? How could she die and leave me all alone. She had no right, goddamn it!"

His hands were bone white as he gripped the branch. The raw anguish in his voice made her steal a glance at him to see his face tight with rage and pain.

"You want her to be there so you can shake her and tell her that she hurt you, that she was selfish. That she had no right to leave you. And then you realize it's forever. She'll never be there again." As he stared off sightlessly across the water, the passion died away, and his voice became low and dead. "And then you cry."

He was a blur beside her now as the tears spilled out, pouring down her cheeks. Tears for her own broken self; tears for Sam, for the pain in his thickened voice.

"And then there are all the firsts. The first birthday, yours and hers. The first Thanksgiving. The first Christmas." His voice cracked. "How does it feel to be under that cold snow for the first time, Robyn?

"The first spring, when the trees bloom anyway. Don't they know that your whole life has been turned upside down, that it'll never be the same again? But life goes on, and it seems for a while that it goes on without you."

She couldn't bear the aching sadness. The silent tears choked her and made her throat ache.

"And then all those well-meaning friends who say, 'Sam, you poor fellow, I know how you must feel, call if you need anything,' while you wander around in your own private hell." His voice dropped almost to a whisper. "Yeah, I know all about it."

Slowly he turned to look at her and she saw the wetness in his reddened eyes.

"Oh, Sam . . . Sam." The salty tears ran down her cheeks into her mouth. "At least she had you. You made her happy. So many people go through life never knowing that kind of happiness. . . ."

"Emma, I miss her so much—" His voice broke and her heart broke for him.

More than anything she wanted to comfort him, soothe him. Reaching out, she put her arms around his neck and with trembling, tentative lips touched his mouth—once, twice.

He gave a deep, anguished groan and pulled her tight against him in a crushing kiss, their tears mingling as she tasted the salt on her lips. Then he pulled back and buried his wet face in her neck, holding her as if he never wanted to let her go.

She clung to him, wanting desperately to believe in the safety of his arms. Wondering who he was holding, and afraid that it was Robyn.

After a time, he raised his head and gently held her a little away from him. Putting a hand under her chin, he tilted her face until she met his gaze. Her heart ached with tenderness to see the streak of tears on his cheeks, the gentleness and understanding in his eyes.

He gave her a small smile. "You look all done in."

She smiled back. "Thanks. That's not a very flattering thing to say to a woman in my position." She wiped at her cheek and tried to laugh. "Now, if this were one of your movies, I would come out looking ravishing, in spite of the tears...."

He touched a gentle finger against her lips, his eyes filled with something deep and serious. "You do. You're a beautiful woman, inside and out."

She could only gaze up at him, lost for words.

"Why don't you get an early night," he said softly. "You've been burning the candle at both ends lately and I think it's catching up with you."

"How do you know?"

He gave her a crooked smile. "I spend a lot of evenings looking up at your window. Either you sleep with your lights on, or you're up working."

"A woman has to make a living. What about you? You must be getting very little sleep, too."

"Yes, but for very different reasons." His expression left her in no doubt what those reasons were, but she had no chance to reply. He turned her around and gave her a little push. "Now scoot."

And she did, feeling more disturbed and dissatisfied than she could ever remember. At the top of the porch steps she turned to see him standing at the water's edge, bathed in the fiery glow of the sunset, his hands shoved in his pockets. There was something in the lines of his body, in the weary stoop of his shoulders, that reached her, deep inside. Something so profound and moving that she knew she would never be the same again.

Inside the house it was still and hot. The ceiling fans hardly stirred the torpid air and the advancing storm clouds soon covered the sky, bringing darkness early.

Emma wandered through the rooms like a restless spirit, confused, churned up, her emotions tumbled and tossed like the trees outside bending to the surging wind.

In her office she clicked on the desk lamp and switched on the computer, then almost immediately switched it off again. She took a pen and legal pad over to the couch, but just sat there, chewing on the tip of her pen. Her whole life was disrupted and confused.

Through the open French doors a livid flare of lightning split the dark sky for an instant, and she counted the seconds before the rumble of far-off thunder. The air hung thick and heavy, so swollen with moisture she could hardly pull it into her lungs.

And then the rain began, the first huge drops splattering down through the maples, onto the honeysuckle and the wild brier rose, then splashing onto the veranda.

Emma flung the pad and pen onto the coffee table, got up and stood in front of the window to stare out into the wild darkness and feel the wind blow her hair back off her hot, damp skin.

She couldn't bear it any longer. Couldn't bear being alone anymore. This restless hunger was gnawing away at her until she thought she'd go mad. Every fibre of her body was crying out and she so yearned to give in.

"Sam," she whispered into the raging night. She wanted Sam.

9

EMMA STEPPED OUT into the cool rain like a person in a trance. *Don't think. Just do it.* Within seconds the downpour drenched her to the skin.

She knocked at the door of the cabin. A moment later it swung open and Sam stared at her in astonishment.

"It's you!" He gave a small bemused laugh. Clearly she was the last person he expected to see on his doorstep. Then his brow furrowed. "Emma, what's wrong? What's happened?"

"Sam, I . . ." she stopped, floundered. "I . . ." Like a person in a dream she raised her hand to wipe the dripping hair back off her forehead, her eyes never leaving his face.

He looked puzzled, but suddenly he seemed to come to himself. "Hey, don't stand out there, you're getting soaked. Get in here." He jerked a thumb toward the interior.

The rain was beating on her back, plastering her hair to her skull, running into her eyes, but she felt paralyzed. Just looking at him, so vital, so masculine, pulled on something deep inside with a power that frightened her.

"For God's sake, Emma, what are you trying to do, catch your death of cold?" Sure enough, she had begun to shiver uncontrollably. He reached out and she allowed him to pull her into the little cabin. A small fire was blazing in the grate and he drew her toward the warmth. "Here, let's get you dried off. Don't you know better than to go running around in this kind of weather?"

Grabbing a towel slung over a nearby chair, he draped it over her head and began patting her face dry and rubbing a her dripping strands of hair. She just stood there and let him, her teeth chattering and her whole body shivering convulsively. But she wasn't cold.

Emma took a deep breath. She could do this. After all, plenty of other people managed this sort of thing without getting all tied up in emotional knots.

"I've been thinking it over, and you're right." Was that strange tentative voice really hers? With great difficulty she tried to sound forceful and assured. "Let's just do it."

Sam stopped toweling her hair and looked at her, his puzzled eyes searching her face. "Let's just do what?"

"Let's just have sex and get it over and done with."

He expelled his breath in disbelief and ran a hand through his hair with a small uncertain laugh.

It had been hard enough to say the words, but whatever reaction she'd expected from him, that wasn't it. "What's the matter? You haven't changed your mind, have you?"

His eyes narrowed and the tiny furrows between his brows deepened. "Yes. I mean, no. I mean . . ." He backed away toward the fireplace. "This is all rather sudden, isn't it?"

She dragged off the towel. This already felt like a bad dream, but she'd come too far to back out now. Besides, she wanted him so badly that it hurt. She couldn't possibly leave until he did something about the state she was in.

She laughed with no real humor. "Well, hardly. You've been trying to convince me almost from the very beginning. I've just decided that you're right. So let's do it."

Her fingers fumbled at the top button of her soggy shirt, flicked it open and slipped down to the next, but Sam put his hand on hers to stop her.

"Just a minute."

"What's the matter? I thought this is what you wanted." Oh, God, this couldn't be happening to her. Not now. Not when she thought she'd die from frustration.

He looked confused and uncomfortable. "I do, but this is rather sudden. You just come marching in here out of the rain and tell me you want to ... do it, just like that."

"You ... you've changed your mind." Confusion and embarrassment overwhelmed her as the momentum ebbed away. For the first time she stopped to think about what she was doing, and the enormity of it suddenly came home to her.

"No, I haven't changed my mind." A slight flush edged his cheekbones and she realized he was trying not to look at her breasts outlined by the drenched shirt. "But you can't just cold-bloodedly tell me you're ready and that I should be ready, too. We should lead up to this. Maybe spend the evening together, have a nice dinner or—"

"What for? We both know what we want. We both know what this has been all about. Is it really necessary to go through all that ritual?"

For a moment he seemed at a loss for words. "I ... I'm not just going to *have sex*."

"Why not? What kind of hypocrite are you? That's what you said, isn't that what you meant?"

"Yes ... no! Let's ... let's talk—"

"Why do we have to talk? You're right. It *is* all about sex, so let's get it over and done with."

"Would you stop saying that! 'Get it over and done with,'" he repeated with distaste, then swore with feeling. "I'm not a barnyard animal! I don't perform on command."

"Look. The smartest thing you ever said was, 'it's just sex. Let's get it out of our systems and get on with it.' Now, what are you saying?"

"I'm saying let's take it slowly. Let nature take its course...."

"Why?" Her voice tightened.

"It's ... it's more romantic."

She gave an angry snort. "Who's talking about romance?"

"I am. I mean, this is not just about sex."

"Then what is it about? You said that it was just a physical attraction and if we slept together it would go away. So let's just sleep together."

"It's not just a physical attraction. Not for me." His voice softened with a deeper, meaningful note. "I feel something for you. I think I'm falling in love."

Every muscle tightened with the familiar fear. "Stop right there. I don't want to hear about love. Let's not cloud the issue."

"Well, I'm sorry. I don't see it that way."

"Oh, great. I can't believe this is happening." She shook her head with a mirthless gasp of laughter, bitter with frustration. "It seems I can't do anything right. Not even a simple affair."

She turned away toward the door, her cheeks burning. Furious with herself, furious with Sam for leading her into this humiliating situation. She wished she were dead.

"Wait, Emma, don't leave." His hand closed over her wrist.

"Let go of me, Sam, just leave me alone." She shook off his grip. "I'm embarrassed enough."

"I didn't mean to embarrass you."

"Please, I don't want to hear it." She turned away from him as tears stung the backs of her eyes. She lunged for the door, but he moved quickly to stand in her way.

"You can't just leave. We have too much to talk about."

She backed away. "I don't think there's anything you could possibly say that would make any difference."

"How about, I love you?"

She shook her head wildly. "Oh no, not that. Wrong answer. I don't need to be told that stupid lie!"

"It's not a lie," he said urgently.

"It is. You've been playing games with me all along. Wanting to see if you could bring me to my knees. Wanting to see me begging for it. Well, are you satisfied?" She hardly knew what she was saying, she just knew she had to escape. But he was barring her way.

Desperate, she turned and bolted out the open sliding door onto the deck. A dark gray curtain of rain slammed into her, drenching her instantly as she leaped toward the railing, intending to swing over and drop into the shallow water where waves crashed and foamed on the shingle four feet below.

Strong hands grabbed her by the waist, hauled her back down and turned her around.

"For God's sake, you've got this all wrong!" he yelled above the roar of the wind and the waves, the rain running down his face.

She struggled in his grip. "Let me go," she sobbed. "I made a mistake, I made a fool of myself. Can't you let me go?" Crying from pain and humiliation, she twisted wildly, trying to get free of his arms.

"No. No, I can't, not like this."

"Why not? You don't want me, you've made that very clear." She didn't know if she made any sense, didn't care as she thrashed wildly in his arms.

"Does this look like I don't want you?" Sam pulled her close, trapping her against his strong body to stop her moving, and then his hot mouth was on hers, kissing her hard and recklessly.

After a last desperate, futile attempt to break free, the frenzied need couldn't be contained any longer, exploding inside her, and she kissed him back with a hunger so painful that it frightened her.

Sam dragged his mouth away to take a deep labored breath, but she couldn't stop. She kissed his throat and his chest, wrapping her hand around his nape in the effort to bring his lips back to her avid mouth.

"You're a crazy woman," he moaned. "You make *me* crazy. I don't know what I want anymore, I don't know what I'm doing. I don't know myself anymore." He punctuated every breathless word with mad, feverish kisses. "There's only one thing I know for sure. If I don't have you, if I don't make love to you right now, I'm going to die."

"Then do it, damn it, just do it!"

His mouth found hers again, hungrily, frantically drinking her in as if he could never get enough. And something snapped inside her, washing away everything but the reality of now, this instant. She needed him as she had never needed anything before.

Desperately she began unbuttoning his sodden shirt, tugging at it impatiently, wanting to feel his naked flesh against her. Flesh she'd dreamed about for so many tortured nights.

He pulled away from her a fraction. "Emma, let's go inside."

"Don't stop," she gasped, every inch of her throbbing now for his touch, avid to feel him, to satisfy the voracious need raging out of control.

She curved a hand around his neck and pulled him back to her, plunging her tongue into his mouth for the sweet, hot taste of him, pulling at the waistband of his shorts with the other hand. She didn't want to think, didn't want to pause an instant, just fill the clutching emptiness inside her, make the ache of wanting him go away.

"This is insane," Sam groaned into her mouth, even as he dragged off her clothing, leaving them both naked to the pounding rain, their sighs and moans washed away in the heavy curtain of water.

The wooden railing pressed into her back, but she was lost to everything but the feeling of wet, slick flesh on flesh, his hot mouth on her throat, on her breasts. Her head fell back with a gasp as his urgent, almost-painful sucking sent a sweet, hot arrow straight down inside her, feeding the burning ache that cried out to be assuaged.

"Don't stop, don't stop," Emma cried, wrapping one leg around him and urging her hips against his.

She was beyond shame, beyond awareness, her blood pulsing with the same wild, elemental force as the lashing of the rain and the crashing fury of the water below. All she knew was the primitive, carnal need to feel him inside her.

"God, Emma, this is crazy." Sam shuddered and she knew the last of his self-control had deserted him.

She hung on to his neck as he picked her up completely off the ground. Wrapping the other leg around him, she felt his hands curve around her buttocks and hold her steady for an instant as he slid into her, piercing to the very core of that aching need.

A gasp escaped her at the instant of pure ecstasy as he filled her. "That feels so good. Oh, it's been so long."

But the mounting, insistent throb would not be denied. She pressed closer, to feel him more completely, feel the depth of his desire. He lifted her slightly to rest her hips on the railing, his breath coming fast, his chest rising and falling rapidly.

"This is a hell of a place to do this. You might fall," he muttered, but he was moving, in long, slow, blissfully powerful strokes that sent the delicious agony spiraling rapidly out of control.

"I don't care. Don't stop now, Sam, don't." She smothered a cry against the slick flesh of his shoulder, sinking her teeth into him, dimly aware of him groaning her name. So close now, so close she could feel it coming, like a volcanic tidal wave from deep inside.

On the crest of the wave she raised her head. The light from the cabin bronzed his wet skin, sculpting his face into powerful planes and inky shadows. She stared into the startling blue of his blazing eyes, saw the thick, dark lashes clumped together with rain. And then it was upon her, overtaking her. Her head fell back as release shuddered through her, wave upon wave rolling over her, tearing wordless cries and moans from her throat. His hot mouth was on her neck and he jerked wildly, his arms tightening convulsively as he emptied himself into her for one glorious eternity.

Suddenly everything stilled. There was only the insistent rush of the waves and the rain drumming on the deck, on the water below and splashing off their bodies.

Slowly Emma raised her head and saw his closed eyes, the expression between pain and ecstasy as he crooned softly, "My darling girl," running his hands down her back, enveloping her in a warmth that was more than just physical. "I want to hold you forever."

Still wrapped around him, she clung tightly and buried her face in his neck, brushing her lips over the faint marks her teeth had left. Conscious of every tiny detail, she could feel his breathing start to slow. The rain beating on her head and back, the subtle pressure and tension of every muscle in his chest and torso, the way his buttocks flexed against her feet as he balanced her weight, the feel of him stirring inside her.

He chuckled and kissed the side of her cheek, his lips gently clinging. "I love you," he murmured, his breath warm against her ear through the cool rain.

With her face still buried in his shoulder she put her fingers to his lips and shook her head. "No." She didn't want to hear that. "Don't spoil it."

He sighed, but didn't argue. Instead, he picked her up and carried her inside, through the living area into the bathroom, stepping straight into the shower stall. After putting her down, he turned on the water.

The spell was broken, and now that it was over she could barely look at him when he turned back to her with a lazy, satisfied smile. "Are you all right?"

"Yes, I'm fine." She was still reeling, her legs still trembling.

"Just fine?" he teased. "I'll have to see if I can do better, won't I?" He backed her up against the wall and his lips came down on hers as he slowly slid into her again. Never in all her years as a married woman had she experienced anything close to what was happening between them.

When her legs wouldn't support her any longer he sank to his knees, bringing her with him, never losing contact, and there on the shower floor with the warm water cascading down around them, she came again, held in Sam's strong arms.

Afterward, he gently began washing her, lathering soap over her shoulders and down to the curve of her breasts.

Confused and shy of her nakedness, she tried to take the soap from his hand. "I can do that."

"I know, but let me."

Turning her back to him, she closed her eyes as he washed her all over, his hands lingering on her breasts, then between her legs, starting the burning torment all over again.

What happened now? This couldn't go on, it was too overpowering. But heaven help her, she wanted him again right now. Instead, she rinsed her body while he washed himself. The few times she darted a glance toward him, his smile was loving and gentle and slightly possessive.

He stepped out first, but before he closed the pebbled glass door he said, "I'll leave you my bathrobe."

She murmured her thanks, taking her time as she waited for him to dry himself and leave the room. She took as long as possible toweling off. But she couldn't put it off forever and finally emerged to discover he'd thrown another log on the fire and had hung her wet clothes over the backs of two wooden chairs to dry. The heat wave seemed to have broken with the storm front, leaving the air cool and damp, so she was glad of the fire's warmth.

Wearing clean, dry shorts Sam stepped out of the tiny kitchen nook and handed her a steaming cup. "Here. I thought maybe you'd like some coffee."

She clutched the bathrobe tighter and took the mug stiffly. "I think maybe I should go home."

"Wait till the rain stops. Your clothes aren't dry yet, anyway. Come and sit down and relax."

Reluctantly she sank down cross-legged on the carpet in front of the fireplace, cradling her cup, self-conscious and unsure, part of her still filled with the wonder of what had happened. She glanced around the familiar room and noticed that he'd made even the temporary residence uniquely his own. A shirt tossed over the back of the chair, a car-rally magazine on the table by the couch.

Sinking down behind her, Sam tried to draw her back into his arms, but she stiffened.

"I'm not going to hurt you," he said quietly. "I just want to hold you."

She leaned back tentatively, ready to spring away.

"Relax," he murmured, nestling her against his shoulder. "Are you all right?" She nodded. "Did I hurt you?" She shook her head.

"Are you regretting it?" Again she shook her head, and heard him let out a long breath of relief. "Good, I'm glad. Maybe we should talk about where we go from here."

She tensed. "What do you mean, 'Where we go from here'?"

"I mean, this is just the beginning."

"Wait a minute, Sam." She sat a little more upright and turned her head so she could see him. "We're just talking a sexual relationship, right? That's what you said, and that's all it is. In a few more weeks you'll be gone and it'll be over."

Uncurling her legs, she moved away to face him and took a deep, shuddery breath. "You don't need to commit yourself to me beyond that. I don't expect it, don't want it."

"Whoa there! You're way ahead of me. Who's talking about commitment? Let's start with spending some time just getting to know each other."

"We are spending time."

He made an impatient sound. "I don't just mean a few weeks. Come back to L.A. with me."

She dropped her gaze, not wanting him to see the fear and confusion that might be betrayed by her eyes. "I can't."

"Why not? It could be fun," he coaxed. "You could come and stay with me, be my guest for a change."

"I don't think so. I don't think I'd like L.A."

"How do you know? You've never been there, have you?" She shook her head. "Besides, we're going to start filming soon. You'll have to be present on the set. I can guarantee there'll be rewrites."

"You can cope with those. You don't need me."

"That's the problem, I do. I do need you."

He reached out and captured her hands, lifting them to his mouth where he began slowly kissing the tips of her fingers, one at a time. The tingling vibrated all the way down to her toes. "Please, come with me."

"No, Sam." She pulled her hands away and clasped them together. "Don't ask me. I can't."

"You mean, you won't." His face hardened with frustration.

"You're just trying to complicate things. Can't we enjoy the time we have here?"

"And then when it's over, what then? I'm not interested in living on memories, Emma."

"I'm sure you'll forget soon enough. After all, this is no different."

He went still and his voice was ominously quiet. "From what?"

"From any other affair you've had."

"How do you know I've had other affairs?"

Her cheeks were warm and the fire suddenly felt hot at her back. "I've read—"

"Oh, yes, that's right, your favorite source," he said bitterly. "Those wonderfully revealing articles."

"What about the Academy Awards last year? I saw you there on TV, with Melissa Fox." The actress's name rolled off her lips with a sneer of pure cattiness that astonished her. "You had your arm around her and you were smiling down at her in the most nauseating way."

The thought of Sam making love to anyone else the way he made love to her made her stomach churn with jealousy. She wrapped the robe tighter and huddled inside it.

Sam raked one hand through his hair in exasperation. "You know, I thought you were smarter than that. Seems I've been wrong. About a lot of things."

"Yes, you are. I think you're confusing love with sex."

She was still doing it, still treating him like some dumb stud with his brain between his legs.

"I know what I feel," he ground out through gritted teeth. "And what I feel for you is love."

She shook back her long, damp curls with a humorless laugh and a depth of bitterness in her eyes that disturbed him. "I don't think either you or I can know what love really is."

"Hey, speak for yourself. You're the one who's confused around here."

"Oh, really?" Emma's dark brows rose in a cynical curve. "Well, then, what is this thing you call love? Only one year after your wife dies you're ready to just forget all about her and fall in love with someone else? How could you forget about her so quickly?"

"You've got it all wrong, Emma." How could he make her understand? "My love for Robyn will never die. She'll always have a part of my heart, but it doesn't mean I'm not capable of loving again as deeply and completely."

"Well, I don't believe in it. Larry said he loved me and he—" She stopped, stricken, and quickly looked away, but not before he saw the tears spring into her eyes.

"And he died." Sam completed the sentence softly. "He didn't want to die. He didn't want to leave you. Don't you see?" He sighed with frustration. "You have so much living ahead of you, Emma. Don't condemn yourself to a life without love."

"I don't want to talk about this anymore." She got to her feet, white and trembling. "There's always a price to pay, isn't there? Well, I've paid my dues, and I'll never make that mistake again."

He stared at her for a long second, then gave a small derisive laugh. "You're right. Maybe there is nothing to talk about. I thought we were on the same wavelength, the same kind of people, but I was wrong. Wrong about you."

"Yes, you were. You were wrong if you thought I was looking for a man to make things right again. I'm not. I'm happy with my life as it is, do you understand? *H-a-p-p-y.* Happy."

"Oh, yes, I understand. You don't need anybody. Lucky you," he sneered. "Well, I'm not ashamed to admit that I need someone to love, someone to love me. And if you were honest with yourself, which you're not, you'd see that you need love, too."

"What do you know about my needs? What do you know about me?"

"Nothing." He heaved a deep breath. "Nothing. I'm sorry. I just assumed we were alike. My mistake. I won't bother you with any of this again."

Emma told herself to be glad that he saw things her way, but that didn't account for the sudden depression that settled on her like a heavy weight.

"The rain has stopped. It's time for me to go home."

"Yes. It's late and I'm tired."

Night had fallen while they weren't looking. Maybe finally tonight she'd be able to sleep. They had done it. They had had sex. Now, perhaps, this consuming fever had worked its way out of her system. It was time to go home and check back into reality.

THE LUMINOUS DIAL on her bedside clock said midnight, and sleep had never been further away. She threw back the sheets and went to look down for the hundredth time at the dim glow of light coming from the cabin window.

What was happening to her? What was this humming awareness permeating her body, making the friction of the cool sheets unbearable because it wasn't the touch of Sam's warm hands, his hungry mouth. She squirmed, trying to block out the rush of arousal, the memory of that madness this evening.

It was just sex. A simple bodily appetite. After two years, it stood to reason that her body wasn't going to be satisfied so soon.

And maybe she'd been right about getting the sickness out of her system. She hadn't thought about Larry even once while she and Sam were together. Those horrible images had stayed buried.

She turned from the window and went quickly downstairs in the T-shirt and underwear she had worn to bed. What if he wasn't interested? He probably wouldn't be, after their parting conversation. The potential for humiliation made her shudder, but she couldn't go on like this.

She angrily slammed the kitchen door behind her and headed down the steps, her bare feet silent on the damp grass. Whatever it took, she *had* to get him out of her system.

It had nothing to do with the fact that she just wanted to feel his arms around her again, feel his tenderness surrounding her, keeping her warm and safe. Those kinds of feelings couldn't be trusted. The safety was just an illusion. Better to know it for what it was. A pure, simple, animal need.

The clouds had blown away and the full moon shone down from a navy sky, dappling the ground under the trees and spreading a shining path on the water. The night air was cool and damp, and she shivered in the thin T-shirt.

At the cabin door she knocked, but got no answer. A light was still glowing inside, though.

She leaned over the porch rail, looked in through the window by the door and her breath caught in her throat. There he was, stretched out on the carpet in front of the fire, beautifully, unashamedly naked, and fast asleep.

A white-hot surge of desire raced through her. Softly she opened the door and crossed the room to where he lay. Sinking to her knees at his side, she gazed at him hungrily. She should leave, but she couldn't bring herself to do it. Surely there was no harm in just looking.

The smooth planes of his face caught the waning firelight and the thick, dark lashes cast shadows on his cheekbones. He slept with one arm flung out and the other hand splayed across his chest, sculpted and golden in the firelight. One knee was slightly drawn up, as if to shelter the cluster of dark curls and his penis lying partly erect against his hard, flat stomach.

She licked her suddenly dry lips and her fingertips trembled with the urge to brush lightly over his smooth skin, to explore the muscular curves and hollows of his body at her pleasure, while he slept on, unaware.

Leaning on one elbow she lowered her face to his. His mouth looked so vulnerable, and she wanted so much to kiss it.

She brushed her lips against his with a feather-light touch and felt no response. He must be sleeping deeply. Some instinct urged her to trail the butterfly kiss over the clean curve of his jaw, to breathe him in as she nuzzled into the hollow of his throat, to find his flat nipple and gently rub her lips across the bead of dark flesh. His chest rose and fell in a small sigh, but he didn't move.

Her lips were tingling, her breasts felt full and heavy as she bent over him, the tight peaks lightly brushing against him through the thin shirt every time she moved.

She trailed the kiss lower, letting her hair whisper across his bare skin, lightly dipping her tongue into his navel. Trembling, she brushed her lips against his satin hardness, and without even thinking, languidly caressed the side of his shaft with her tongue.

He moaned and moved a little. She swiftly looked up to his face, but his eyes were still closed. This was wanton and shameless, she shouldn't be doing it, but she couldn't stop. She didn't want to stop. Between her thighs she felt hot and wet and swollen with the ache of wanting.

Bending her head again, she opened her mouth and gently took him in. He gave a small twitch and she heard his breath catch, heard him gasp her name in a hoarse, throaty croak. She paused for a moment, then continued, until his fingers threaded through her hair and the pressure of his hands stilled her head.

"What are you doing?" He jerked up to sitting position as she drew back from him a little.

"I want to have sex again." Her voice was husky and demanding and nothing at all like herself.

He wiped a hand over his face, then looked at her. His eyes still a little unfocused from sleep, slowly his expression sharpened until it became searchingly acute.

He took a deep breath and slowly exhaled. "No." A small gasp escaped her, then he continued. "But I'll make love with you if you want." His cheeks were flushed, his eyes were burning, reflecting the desire that threatened to devour her.

Relief washed over her. "Call it what you want, let's just do it." She reached for him, but he grasped her arms and held her away from him.

"Not till you ask me to make *love* with you."

"This is silly."

He pulled her down on top of him and nudged his hard length against her, where she was aching for him to be. She gave a little moan and tried to increase the pressure, but he shifted and wouldn't let her. "No, it's not. It's blackmail."

"You should be ashamed to admit it," she moaned.

"The words, Emma. The words." He deliberately brought his thigh up between her legs and applied a slight pressure. "Is it so difficult?"

"You're a low-down, filthy, double-crossing son of a bitch," she spat out.

"Those aren't quite the words I had in mind," he said with a breathless chuckle.

She would have given anything to be able to get up and walk away. She hated being forced into submission by her own weakness, her own need, but she was melting for him; it was becoming intolerable.

Finally she had to gasp out the words. "Please . . . please make love with me."

His blue eyes glittered and his mouth curved in a demonic smile of triumph as he pulled her down and rolled over so that he was on top of her. "I thought you'd never ask."

10

SOMETHING WAS PRESSING uncomfortably against her forehead and she was lying on an awfully hard surface, Emma thought, as she swam back to consciousness.

She opened her eyes to find herself lying half off the futon in the cabin loft, with the bare boards beneath her and her face pressed up to the leg of the dresser.

Rolling up on one elbow, she cast around with bleary eyes at what looked like a war zone. The small lamp from the dresser lay on the floor, its parchment shade dented, along with a dressing case of Sam's, the contents strewn all over. Sheets and pillows were scattered everywhere and even the pictures on the walls hung askew, as if the place had been hit by an earthquake.

She closed her eyes again and groaned. An earthquake was as good a way as any to describe the wild, tempestuous night that had only ended when exhaustion claimed them both, about the time the sky had begun fading into gray. Could that really have been her—that abandoned, licentious creature?

Even then, she'd wanted to go home, but Sam wouldn't let her. "What kind of a guy do you think I am?" he'd said. "You make me feel so cheap." He'd been teasing, but he was utterly serious in his intention because his smile had soon vanished and his blue eyes darkened with emotion. "Come on, Emma, stay. Let me hold you, I need to feel you close."

In spite of herself his husky pleading was hard to resist. Then he'd pulled her back into his arms, wrapping himself around her from behind as she lay there, stiff and tense.

"Relax," he'd murmured, sleepily content. "Mmm, this is nice. I feel I've been doing this with you forever."

That was the problem. It had felt nice. Wonderful, in fact. So warm and safe. And she didn't want to trust that feeling for an instant; it could be too cruelly deceiving. She didn't want to get used to the blissful contentment that stole over her, making her spent muscles relax against the cradle of his warm, strong body, even as her mind warned her that she was heading into dangerous territory.

And now in the dull gray light of dawn she sat up and looked at Sam. He still lay on the futon, sprawled out on his back, naked but for a narrow swath of sheet lying across his hips; and she could see that he was hard. Again the heat flooded through her. Again the surge of wanting rose up like a fierce hunger inside. A hunger that she was beginning to fear could never be appeased.

It wasn't right. It wasn't healthy, to be so insatiable. How could she want him again when she still ached from last night?

Forcing herself to look away from him, she crept off the futon and went quietly down the narrow loft stairs. She slipped on her long T-shirt, gave up on finding her underwear, and let herself out into the cool light of dawn.

Back in her own kitchen she went through the automatic ritual of filling the kettle and plugging it in. She made the tea and left it to steep, then trod wearily upstairs.

She stepped into a hot shower, conscious of the aches and little throbbing sensations in the most intimate places—tangible proof of that torrid night, in case she doubted her own vivid memories. But she couldn't stop remembering. Couldn't erase the feel of his hands, the taste of his flesh, the way he'd made her feel so . . . special.

Leaning back she closed her eyes and let the water run over her face with a sigh of satisfaction. She'd never experienced anything like last night in her whole life. Why not admit to herself that it had been incredible?

Maybe she'd finally grown up, become like all those other people who took what they wanted and satisfied their sexual needs the way they'd satisfy any other appetite, without becoming emotionally scarred or dependant.

For the first time in what seemed like a lifetime, she felt a sense of hope. Those nightmare images had never recurred. Perhaps, finally, she wasn't pretending anymore; perhaps she was really becoming the tough new woman she wanted to be. Someone who wouldn't be taken advantage of so easily. A woman who could satisfy her needs and then get on with business.

Turning off the shower, she wrapped herself in a towel, pushed aside the curtain and stepped out of the tub. And there was Sam, sitting on the edge of her bed, with a smile on his face that could melt tar.

He was barefoot, in shorts and a loose cotton shirt, unbuttoned all the way. He looked disturbingly at home as he sat there so relaxed, a mug of tea cradled in his hands between spread thighs.

"I brought you a cup." He nodded toward the steaming mug on the bedside table, but his gaze never left her for an instant as she paused on the threshold. And the smile in his eyes was so warm and full of shared intimate knowledge that she could feel her breasts growing swollen and heavy, feel her nipples hardening in response to that scorching look. "You know what I was thinking?"

She stepped over and reached for her cup, but quickly moved away from him toward the end of the bed. "What were you thinking?"

"I was thinking we should take the day off. Spend some time together having fun."

She turned and walked over to look out the window, gripping her cup tightly. "That doesn't sound like a very responsible thing to do."

That invigorating sense of confidence and control had fled like the morning mist in the sunlight. Just his presence here in her room, so undeniably, so attractively male, turned her into a mass of quivering nerve ends, not a rational, thinking being.

"So let's be irresponsible." He was smiling that wicked smile. She could hear it in his voice.

"What about your schedule?"

She mustered the nerve to turn and face him and found he had stretched out on his stomach across her bed, and lay looking at her with his chin propped on one hand and, sure enough, that devastating smile on his lips.

"We're way ahead. And besides, who gives a damn about that?" His voice shimmered with sultry, husky promise. "I want to be with you. I want to spend the day indulging every sexual fantasy I've had about you." He reached out and ran his fingertip down the length of her exposed thigh below the towel.

Her legs quivered and threatened to give way beneath her. He was taking this too far, too fast, and she was disturbed by how much it excited her.

"That would be a shocking waste of time," she managed to reply, her voice thready.

He ignored her feeble protest. "And when I'm done, you can indulge every sexual fantasy you've had about me."

"Well, that should take all of five minutes." As an attempt to be flippant, it failed miserably. Her heart was pounding so hard she couldn't catch her breath.

"Bull."

"What do you mean, bull?" She was beginning to panic. This was getting out of hand.

"I mean, you go up in flames when I touch you. You can't even look at me without wanting me."

"You just think you're irresistible, don't you?"

"Aren't I?"

"No."

"Well, let's see if you can resist this." Suddenly he grabbed the corner of her towel and yanked.

"You're going to spill my tea!" Emma yelped as she lost her balance, barely managing to set the cup on the dresser beside her. The towel went sailing through the air as she toppled onto the bed.

"Stop it, Sam," she gasped out.

Quick as lightning, Sam rolled over, wrapping his arms around her hips so that she couldn't move and burying his face between her legs.

"What are you doing?"

"I'm having breakfast," his muffled voice came to her. The first touch of his tongue sent a searing jolt of sensation right down to her toes.

"I don't have time for this!" she cried, as her hands curled into the sheets in a death grip. She clamped her teeth together to strangle the moan welling up in her throat as her body melted.

"Shut up and let me eat in peace, will ya!"

"MMM...MMM...GOOD. Did you make these?" Sam asked, through a mouthful of blueberry muffin.

"Fritz did. I don't bake very well, I'm afraid."

"Never mind, you have hidden talents." The scorching look in his eyes brought a hot flush to her cheeks. "And I want to discover them all over again."

"Haven't you had enough?"

"Uh-uh . . . Have you?"

She looked away, feeling the heat rise in her cheeks. When would it ever be enough? When would she ever feel complete? The more they did it, the more she wanted, the more unfulfilled she felt. It didn't make sense. What was she reaching for?

He put his fingers under her chin and gently turned her head to look at him, tweaking her slightly when she wouldn't meet his eyes, until finally she felt compelled to look up. His smile was gentle and understanding.

"After everything we've shared, is it possible you're still shy of me, Emma?"

She shook her head and smiled. "I just can't believe that we're sitting here on my bed, stark-naked, eating muffins and drinking coffee, like it's the most natural thing in the world to be doing."

"Didn't you and Larry ever have breakfast in bed?" He gave an incredulous laugh.

"Not like this." In all the years with Larry, she'd never done anything so spontaneous.

"I don't believe you."

"He would have been worried about crumbs staining the bed linen, or been in a hurry to get to work. He would never have thought of taking the day off just to spend it making love." Not with her, anyway.

"If you don't mind my saying so, Larry sounds like a bit of a bore."

And suddenly she was amazed to realize that she agreed with him. She'd never thought about it before, but her marriage to Larry had been safe, secure, and terminally dull. But still she felt duty-bound to protest.

"It just seems so hedonistic, so self-indulgent. We've been up here all morning."

He gave her a slow smile that started her blood pounding all over again. "Yeah, and we're going to be up here all afternoon. Unless you're getting bored?"

He set his cup on the bedside table and lay back against the pillows with relaxed masculine grace, and a smile on his lips that should be declared a lethal weapon.

She found herself responding to that licentious curve of his mouth. Why not? After all, was she any different from thousands of other women the world over who felt the same way about that smile? And suddenly it occurred to her that she was. They could only dream and fantasize. She had him here beside her, naked in her bed, wanting her. A reckless, delicious abandonment took hold of her.

"Not yet, but I'll let you know." She smiled, a little shy for all her bold words. But why not indulge herself? At least she wasn't hurting anyone.

"It's been quite a while for you, hasn't it?" His expression had sobered a little and there was a seriousness in his eyes that reached out to her. "There hasn't been anybody since Larry."

"No." She couldn't meet that look and dropped her gaze to the empty paper muffin cup in her hand, folding it over and over on itself.

"I hope you're not feeling guilty about doing this. It's okay. It's normal to need another human being, but it's also normal to feel that you're being unfaithful to Larry. For awhile there, I felt the same way about Robyn. But we're alive, and that's not a crime. We owe it to ourselves to go on living, to be happy. And if we're lucky, to fall in love again. There's nothing wrong with that."

"I don't feel guilty about what I'm doing, but let's not bring love into this. Please, Sam." She didn't know what she felt, except that it was confusing and much too powerful.

She dropped the screwed-up paper onto the plate with the crumbs and turned away to set it on the dresser.

His hand caressed her bare knee—a warm, comforting touch. "It's too late, Emma. I care about you very much. I'm already in love with you."

Her stomach tightened and the old anxiety came surging back, full force. She moved away from his touch, not quite meeting his eyes. "Don't. Don't do this to me. You don't know me, you don't know anything about me, how can you love me? And I don't need to be told these lies."

"What *is* it?" He got up onto his knees on the bed. "What's eating away at you? You've got to let go. You've got to talk about him or you're never going to be whole!"

He was doing it again. Making her feel frantic and trapped. Why couldn't he understand that the past was better buried?

"Why do you need to know everything? Why can't this be enough?" She reached out and ran a hand over his penis.

He grabbed her wrist. "For how long?"

"For however long it lasts."

She moved closer, to kneel between his thighs and put her arms around his neck. "Please, Sam, don't spoil it. Can't we just enjoy the moment?"

The frustration still hardened his face, but he put his arms around her and ran his hands up and down her back as his voice softened a little. "It's not so easy for me, Emma. I'm in love with you."

A small sigh escaped her. Who was he in love with? This empty shell of a woman? The Emma Jordan who had laughed and played in this house as a child, grown up in this town and married in the little church on the hill had ceased to exist two years ago. She had nothing left to offer anyone.

A little push sent him toppling backward onto the pillows and she lay on top of him, moving her hips against his in a slow, rhythmic motion. "Then just make love to me, let me lose myself in this." With a thrill of power she felt him harden in response. "It's all that's real."

She reached down to guide him and let out a little gasp as he slid into her, filling her. "*Yes.* Oh, Sam, I love the feeling of you inside me. Don't you see? The only thing I can count on is right here, right now."

He pushed the hair back off her face, and she could see him struggling for control, shuddering in the grip of desire as he spoke. "You're wrong. This isn't all there is. There's so much more."

She shook her head and gasped out, "It's just an illusion, words that people say." Somewhere deep inside she felt the knife twist again. "But *show* me love. You can't. What is it? Where is it? I can't believe it anymore. I can only believe in what is tangible."

"Then believe this."

He gripped her hard and rolled her over with a kiss, plunging his tongue into her sweet, soft mouth. Whatever it took, he wanted to obliterate all her pain and fear, if only the force of his love could be enough.

"I *am* in love with you, Emma." He knew that now, with every beat of his heart. "But how can I fight a ghost? How can I make you see that your capacity for love didn't die with Larry, no matter how much his death crushed you?"

"Please, Sam, stop talking. None of that matters right now, don't you understand? Just this." Her hands ran frantically over his back, clutching and releasing as she moved beneath him. "This is all that matters."

With a moan she closed her eyes and arched into him. She was still shutting him out. Even while he buried himself in her, she was shutting him out. Anger surged and he despised himself for his weakness.

He shouldn't be allowing her to use him like this, to hide from herself in carnal oblivion, but he couldn't stop himself from responding to her. It would be like trying to make the rain stop falling, or the sun stop shining. But damn it all, what about his self-respect?

He slid out of her, ruthlessly ignoring her gasped protest and the painful response of his body. But he stayed on top, keeping her prisoner. "I think you do care for me, in some way. I'll stake my life on it."

"What makes you so sure?" She tried to turn her head away, but he held it there with his hands cupping both sides of her flushed face.

"Because you're not the kind of woman to give yourself to me like this without feeling something, no matter how hard you try to pretend that it doesn't go more than skin deep. The way you look at me, the way you respond to me, make a lie of the words that come out of your mouth."

"You're wrong. The only thing I feel is horny."

She was so beautiful lying there beneath him, her eyes huge and smoky with wanting him, but still with that lingering hint of buried pain he couldn't erase. Her parted mouth was full and swollen with kisses, and a rosy flush spread from her cheeks down her neck to the curve of her breasts. And under him her body felt so soft, so pliant and giving. God help him, he wanted her so much it hurt.

"You're not a very good liar." The words were shaky and he could feel himself losing the fight. "But we'll argue about that later. Right now, I want you like you want me." He slid back into her waiting warmth.

She closed around him with a small sigh, her voice tight with need. "I won't argue about that."

In spite of his earlier confidence, he just wished he could really be sure that she *did* want him in the same way that he needed her.

But all that was soon forgotten as he moved slowly inside her. She felt so right, so perfect. It was magic. He kissed her satin shoulder and cupped her breast, kneading in gentle rhythm with his movements, teasing the nipple with his thumb. He couldn't resist any longer and lowered his head to take it into his mouth, lost in the taste of her, in the scent of her flesh.

With a moan, she arched toward him while her hands slid down his back to squeeze his buttocks in a hard, convulsive rhythm, bringing both pain and pleasure as her movements matched his slow, deep thrusts.

He kissed a path to her other breast and heard her gasp, "Oh, my darling, that feels so good."

He *knew* it! He knew there was more. Just that simple endearment on her lips flooded his soul with joy and hope. He brought his mouth back to hers. "Say it again, Emma. Say those words again."

Her eyes were glazed and dark as she looked up into his. She hadn't even been aware of what she'd said. Who was she making love to, him or Larry? But even as burning jealousy grabbed him by the throat, everything shattered into blinding oblivion.

Suddenly it didn't matter. Nothing mattered but Emma, here in his arms. And now he couldn't hold out any longer as her head fell back, her movements became strained and frantic, and she began convulsing around him.

"Sam!" she called out in a strangled cry.

"It's me. You're making love to me, not him!" Ecstatic triumph coursed through him like a flash flood through a canyon. He felt himself exploding into her, pouring out every ounce of love he possessed. For that one incredible moment he felt invincible.

He sagged onto her shoulder, burying his face in the soft silk of her hair as they both gasped raggedly for breath. After a moment he rolled off and nestled her into the crook of his shoulder, wrapping his arms around her.

For a long time he lay watching the shifting patterns of the sunlight on the ceiling, listening to her quiet breathing and the gentle splash of the waves on the shore. There were so many unanswered questions, but he wouldn't be robbed of this one perfect moment.

Finally Emma murmured, "Will you come back and visit me?"

He felt a cold chill, despite the sultry air drifting in past the filmy curtains. She was already imagining him gone. "Do you want me to?"

He felt her nod. "Yes."

"Why?"

She gave him a teasing smile. "Because . . . 'I've grown accustomed to your face…'" she sang softly, as her finger trailed lightly across his jaw.

It was a hell of a long way from what he wanted, but it looked like he'd have to be content with that. Anyway, it was a start. "Then I will."

"Sam, about what you said earlier…"

Through the open bedroom doorway he heard noises from downstairs. The sound of the front door opening and then closing again with a decisive click, followed by footsteps in the hall.

Emma slowly sat up and stared at him, wide-eyed.

"Fritz?" he suggested.

"No. Fritz had a doctor's appointment down in the city today." She slid off the bed, took her bathrobe from the peg behind the door and slipped it on.

He had already reached for his shorts and was stepping into them as he caught her questioning look.

"I'm not letting you go down there alone. Could be an intruder."

He followed her quietly down the stairs and into the living room where she came to a dead stop.

Her mother-in-law was just turning away from the fire-place. The landscape that had hung above the mantel was on the floor, leaning against the wall, and in its place hung an oil portrait of a man. A blond, exceptionally handsome man that he knew at once had to be Larry. They must have made a stunning couple. The thought gave him a sharp pang of jealousy. And then it hit him. Emma had no pictures of her husband anywhere in the house.

"Emma, what's he doing here?" His attention came back to the woman now staring at them in shock. Her faded blue eyes darted from Emma to him, taking in the way they were dressed and drawing the obvious conclusion. He saw the swift change in her expression from surprise to outrage. "How could you? Do you have no decency?"

The old battle-ax had her nerve, after waltzing in unin-vited. He was about to weigh in on her when he was stopped in his tracks by the venom in Emma's low, scathing voice.

"How dare you come in here and bring that. How *dare* you!" Rigid and trembling from head to foot, her face as white as death, she balled her hands into fists and screamed, "Get out of my house, do you hear? Get out and take that thing with you!"

Then she whirled around, pushed him out of the way and dashed for the stairs.

11

"SHE'S GONE," he said from the bedroom doorway, not bothering to add that he'd come a hair's breadth from helping her on her way with a swift kick.

Emma swung around from the bay window and the wildness in her eyes shocked him. "You can go, too." Her long dark hair flared out around her chalky face in a tangled halo as she began pacing the room.

"I can't leave you like this." He took a few steps toward her feeling more helpless than he'd ever felt in his whole life.

"You'd better, if you know what's good for you."

"Emma . . ."

"I mean it, Sam. I don't want you. Can't you understand that?" She paused in front of him, her chest heaving under the thin robe, the last of her control about to snap.

"Come on, honey, calm down—"

"Get the hell out of here or I'll hurt you, I swear I will." She put her hands on his chest and pushed, hard.

He braced himself and gritted his teeth. Nothing short of an earthquake was going to move him from this room. "Then hurt me. You have something to get out of your system and if it'll help, then go ahead, hit me."

She dropped her hands and clenched them at her sides, her whole body shaking, her mouth trembling. It killed him to see her like this, but he knew that pain. God, how he knew it.

"Come on, Emma, hit me. I can take it."

Instead, with a frustrated groan she pushed on his chest again, harder this time so that he reeled back a little, but stood his ground.

"I can't stand this anymore...." Her low voice became a shriek of fury.

She spun away from him with a gasp, her cloud of dark hair flying as she scooped up a glass vase of roses from the table by the sofa and with a ferocious groan, hurled it toward the far corner, shattering it into a thousand glittering shards with an explosive crash.

"Don't you understand?" she screamed as she whirled around, furious and frantic, the only color in her white face a hectic slash of red blazing along each cheekbone. "The son of a bitch died!"

"Yes, I understand. And it's time you accepted it, and let go." Calm, he had to keep calm for her sake. Finally, *finally*, she was letting it out.

She lunged toward him, her fists clenched. "Accept it! I've had no choice but to accept it!" The words tore out of her, in strangled sobbing, hysterical laughter that twisted his guts with anguish.

He held out his hands to her, but she groaned and beat them away with her fists. He hardly recognized her as she turned, looking around her frantically, her hands clenching and unclenching until she made a sudden lunge and wrenched a framed print off the wall. She stood for a moment, clutching the picture indecisively. Tears were now pouring down her cheeks and the impotent fury in her stricken face wrenched at his heart, galvanizing him.

"Throw it."

She looked up, startled by his command, as if she'd forgotten he was there.

"This thing has eaten you up long enough." He curled his hands over hers on the edge of the frame. "Now throw it," he repeated.

"Leave me alone, you big jerk, and get out of here." She tried to yank her hands away, but he only tightened his grip.

"Throw it," he growled.

She struggled, but he won. Clutching her hands, he made her lift the picture and dash it hard against the wood floor. With the noise of the splintering frame it was as if a dam had broken.

For a moment she froze, staring at the shattered mess at her feet, then murmured, as if in a dream, "Look what you made me do."

The next instant she suddenly threw back her head and screamed in pain. "I hate him! I hate him!"

He carefully picked up the picture and threw it into the corner with the other broken glass. He didn't want her cutting her feet, but he didn't want to stop her, either.

It was like watching someone else take over Emma's body. His heart was pounding with fear, his mouth went dry. No, he wasn't going to stop her, unless she tried hurting herself.

In a frenzy, she tore around her room pulling pictures off the walls, books out of the bookshelves, throwing every loose object that came to hand and screaming out her fury. Except that now she screamed, "I hate *you*."

Finally the small sitting room was a shambles, but like a creature possessed with a taste for destruction she lunged into the bedroom, yelling, "He had no right to die like that!" She tore the covers off the bed, ripping at the lace coverlet as the anger poured out of her in a hot, molten stream. "No right to die before I had a chance to tell him!"

All the anger that had been corroding inside her was finally coming to the surface. He moved toward her, not ever sure what he was planning to do, but she slammed an arm across his chest, knocking the breath out of him, sending him toppling backward onto the bed. For a moment he lay struggling to get the air back into his lungs. Then he sat up.

"That bastard!" The pure venom in her words chilled him to the bone. "I'm so tired of being the good, dutiful wife and widow." She was starting on the sheets now, and the vicious sound of the ripping cotton seemed to goad her to more destruction. "I'm so tired of hearing what a great man he was, what a wonderful husband he was." She broke into hysterical laughter, but when he reached for her it turned into a moan of fury and she pushed him away savagely. "Don't touch me."

"It's okay, sweetheart." He stood and stepped toward her, reaching out to her, but she backed away. "That's it," he crooned. "Get rid of it. It's been tearing you apart long enough."

But she launched herself furiously at him, sending him toppling back onto the mattress, pounding at him with her fists. He could take it. He'd take anything for her. He'd die for her.

"I hate him. I hate him!"

"That's it, honey, let it all out." He gasped a little at the hail of painful blows. But what were a few bruises compared to the raw, gaping wounds still burning inside her?

But when he went to hold her she whirled away from him. Snatching up her pillow, she tore at the cotton cover and feathers billowed out as she began ripping it apart. "How could he do it? How could he be such a selfish son of a bitch!"

"That's it," he encouraged. "Get it all out. Don't hold back, honey, don't hold back."

She hurled the gutted pillow away and stumbled over to the window, with bitter sobs that seemed to be wrenched from her soul. He could see that she was losing strength, becoming exhausted. But then she seemed to rally with renewed passion.

A savage moan erupted from her as she deliberately wound her hands around the curtain and with one vicious yank tore it away from the rod. It drifted down in filmy folds over the wreckage that had been her lovely bedroom.

She swivelled around, and her eyes lit on the only object left intact. Like a madwoman bent on destruction she lunged for it—a small, blue Depression-glass bowl that sat on her dresser. She picked it up and was about to hurl it at the bathroom door when suddenly all the fight went out of her. Slowly, wearily, she sank down to the carpet, clutching the bowl to her chest, her eyes closed and her head drooping like a wilting flower.

He slid off the bed and onto his knees, looking at her. "Emma?" The hoarse whisper didn't sound like it belonged to him. He held his breath. Now what?

With a deep, shuddering sigh she raised her head and stared at him with shell-shocked eyes, then shifted her gaze slowly around the room at the destruction she had wreaked.

Sam crawled through the litter and sank down anxiously beside her. He took her hand in his. It was cold, almost lifeless and he began chafing her fingers, rubbing warmth into her. He wanted to hold her, wrap her in his arms, but he felt uncertain about what would be best for Emma. What did she want? He raised her fingers to his lips, but the sound of her voice made him freeze in the act.

"When I saw those two policemen standing on the doorstep I knew something had happened," she began, in a dead, expressionless voice, as if she were completely unaware of his presence.

She was talking, finally! He was afraid to breathe in case she stopped.

"When they told me Larry was dead, at first I couldn't take it in. I couldn't believe what was happening." She paused and swallowed, but then continued in that same unemotional tone.

"I was hoping I was just dreaming. But I wasn't. And then there was poor Fritz in the hospital with all those horrible burns to his face. He tried to drag Larry out of the car, you see." Now she did look at him and her voice broke. "He was thrown free, but Larry was trapped behind the wheel. Fritz tried to save him. But it was too late." Again her voice lost all emotion. "Larry was dead.

"I went through the funeral in a kind of daze." She shook her head and closed her eyes, then went on, her voice thick and husky. "We'd been married for ten years. He was my whole world."

A painful lump formed in his throat and he felt the sting of tears in his eyes, but when he reached for her she made a small movement away from him.

Don't take it personally, man. It's Emma that counts.

"It was weeks before I could bring myself to go into his office and sort out his things. I cried the whole time I did it. So many reminders of a life shattered. And yes, I was angry with him for leaving me." She brushed away the tear rolling down her cheek and her voice cracked. "I just didn't know how I was going to go on without him.

"I put everything into a bag and brought it home. That night I cried myself to sleep, holding the picture of us he kept in his office. Why did it have to be him? We were so happy together."

Again she turned and looked at him, her eyes large and vacant, her voice once again empty of all emotion. "We were the perfect couple, you know. Everybody said so. It was such a tragedy. Everybody said so. And I couldn't understand what sort of malevolent god would take him from me." She stopped and shook her head, as if she still couldn't understand.

"A few days later I got around to sorting out the bag I'd brought from the office. He'd had some videotapes in his safe. I couldn't imagine what was on them. Maybe pictures of our last vacation. Larry was camera mad. So I played them." Something hard and bitter in her eyes made his heart contract. "There were six of them. All of Larry and another woman."

"Oh my God!"

The toneless voice continued. She hadn't even heard him. "She was married, too. I saw her ring. I suppose the relationship was ideal for both of them." A small humorless smile curved her lips and a shiver of horror jerked through him. "It certainly lasted a long time. Eight years . . . I could tell by the dates on the tapes."

The horror gave way to cold anger.

"I've never seen any pornographic movies, but I'm sure these would rank right up there. I didn't know so many positions were even possible. I didn't know that Larry was capable of such . . . passion." A flicker of revulsion passed over her face that made his stomach churn and his anger burn even hotter.

"I never thought our sex life was unexciting, until I saw those videos. He was a tender, loving husband and if it lacked spontaneity, it didn't bother me. I didn't expect anything from Larry that I thought he couldn't give." Her mouth hardened with cynical bitterness. "I didn't know, of course, that he was giving at the office."

"Honey, don't—"

"They used to meet on the boat, you see. Of course, I couldn't stand the sight of it anymore. I practically gave it away. I would sooner have burned it." The vicious undertone made him flinch. "I burned those tapes, but they've lived in my head ever since. Every graphic detail. Every passion-filled groan."

"The bastard!" Sam clenched his fists, burning with anger. He wanted to kill the guy for this, kill him all over again.

And then suddenly Emma's face crumpled, tears welled up in her dark eyes and spilled over, rolling down her cheeks. "Why did he do that? Why did he need her? What was wrong with me?" She began to weep—huge, heart-wrenching, hiccuping sobs that seemed to be tearing her apart. "Why wasn't I good enough?"

He wrapped his arms around her and drew her close. He wanted to hold her so tight that nothing could hurt her like that anymore.

"Nothing is wrong with you," he told her fiercely. "Absolutely nothing."

Her shoulders heaved. "Maybe if I'd been—"

"No. No, Emma. Something was wrong with Larry, not with you. You can't blame yourself for what he did."

"Then, why?" she sobbed against his chest. "Why did he do it?"

"I don't know, darling. I don't know why." His own tears were pouring down his face, blinding him, until the world was reduced to the heartbroken woman in his arms. "He must have been crazy."

"Yes, he was crazy, all right...but not about me." Her tears came fresh and hot as she sobbed into him.

He felt so helpless just sitting there holding her, rocking her, crooning gently to her. Finally the storm of weeping subsided, but every few seconds, long shuddering breaths racked her body as he cradled her in his arms.

As the calm descended, and everything she'd told him began to sink in, he suddenly felt the anger rising up in him all over again. "Did you keep this secret for two years? Did you not tell anybody?"

She sniffed and nodded.

"Emma, why? Wasn't there anybody you could talk to?"

"How could I?" Her words were muffled against his chest. "He was dead."

"Yeah, and you didn't even have the chance to confront him. So you bottled up all that anger and blamed yourself." It was all so clear now, so brutally clear.

"I gave him everything and it wasn't enough. I wasn't enough."

Her wet cheek rubbed against his bare chest as she shuddered in his arms, and the tears came again with heartbreaking despair. He swallowed hard, but blinked back the moisture gathering in his eyes again.

"Shh." He stroked her back, rubbed his chin on her silky head. "It's all right, it's not you. You're wonderful, you're beautiful, don't you know that? You make me crazy with desire. I can't imagine wanting anyone else if I had you."

He cradled her in his arms, gently rocking her back and forth, until finally her sobbing died away and she lay limp against him, dragging in shaky breaths.

Tenderly he picked her up and carried her through the debris of her ruined bedroom. He laid her gently on the stripped mattress, smoothed the hair back from her face and found the sheet to pull over her. Lying huddled on the bed, she looked like a lost little girl. Every protective instinct he possessed rose up with an intensity that almost strangled him.

"Why don't you get some sleep," he whispered. "We'll talk some more later." He bent over and placed a gentle kiss on her forehead, but when he went to move away she clutched his hand in panic.

"Please don't go. Don't leave me."

"I won't. I'm here, sweetheart." He lay down beside her and drew her into his arms, curving her head against his shoulder.

"What would I do without you?" she said in an exhausted murmur. "If it hadn't been for you, I'd still be living in hell."

He pulled her tighter, his throat thick and sore. "Shh. Go to sleep." Emma, darling Emma. He could hold her like this till the day he died.

IN THE GRAY LIGHT of dawn Sam eased his arm out from beneath her shoulders. Her face was a pale oval against the white sheets. She still looked drawn, even in sleep, and there were faint purple shadows beneath her eyes.

God knows, he felt like he'd been through the wringer himself. He'd watched her through the night, held her through dark dreams and fearful crying and finally seen her sink into the sleep of utter exhaustion.

Carefully he edged away, swung his feet to the floor and got out of bed. No matter what she said last night, in the light of day things always looked different.

Stepping quietly into the hall, he went downstairs and out to his cabin.

So finally all the pieces that made up the mystery of Emma Jordan had fallen into place. Now he understood, and it all made sense. But something else was clear, too.

The wound had gone so deep it had damn near destroyed her. Last night had been the first step in a long road to healing her battered sense of self-worth. Right now he couldn't expect anything from Emma, except what she was ready to give. And no matter how much it hurt, he had to accept that when she was finally whole she might decide that she didn't want him.

Restless and exhausted, he pulled off his shorts and stepped into a hot shower.

God knows, he wanted her, but only if she loved and wanted him in return. And not because she was confusing gratitude with love. Maybe the best thing he could do for her right now was give her some space, some time to think.

He dried off, threw on a pair of khaki pants and a shirt and stepped out onto the deck. He leaned on the railing and looked out on the lake, still as glass under a pale wash of blue sky. Another hot one today, by the feel of it.

Way out on the water the loon was bobbing and diving. Off toward the marshy side of the point he saw a great heron swooping by, and a flock of killdeer scuttled around on the shore below, digging up bugs like crazy.

The world just kept on turning, didn't it? The circle of life kept coming around. And right now his whole life rested in Emma's hands. He was helpless, and he wouldn't use emotional blackmail to bring her to him. She was too vulnerable. She'd been abused enough by the man in her life and he wouldn't add to her heartache.

He sighed and pushed himself away from the railing. On the way through the cabin he picked up his keys, then closed the door behind him, walked over to the Jeep and drove away.

EMMA SAT UP and looked around the war zone that had been her bedroom. A tornado couldn't have done much more damage. But as she surveyed the sorry wreckage she felt ridiculously light and buoyant and truly glad to be alive for the first time in two long years.

A crippling weight had been lifted from her shoulders and now everything was crystal clear.

"Sam," she whispered to herself, as if even his name was some kind of talisman. "I love you, Sam," she breathed out loud.

Tiptoeing through the debris, she pulled a cotton shift dress from her wardrobe and slipped it on. She couldn't wait to see him, to tell him. Now she understood what had frightened and disturbed her so much. She'd been falling in love with him, and fighting hard against the emotion that had practically destroyed her.

Except that this was different from anything she'd ever felt before. Sam was different.

She ran lightly down the stairs and out of the house, racing barefoot over the cool, wet earth. She couldn't wait to see him, to throw her arms around him, to kiss her thanks for his strength, his tenderness.

Not bothering to knock, she charged into the cabin. "Sam! Where are you?" she called, as she pounded up the stairs. "Oh, darling, I have something so important to tell you."

The loft was empty. She ran back down. Everything looked neat and immaculate. No clothes lying around. No papers or books on the table by the couch. Her heart dropped to her stomach and she felt sick.

Running out onto the front deck, she noticed for the first time that his Jeep was gone.

She sprinted the quarter mile to the gate and met Fritz rolling the lawn mower up toward the house.

"Have you seen Sam?" She stopped and leaned her hands on her knees, gasping for breath.

Fritz was eyeing her with undisguised alarm. "Yes, he drove out of here about an hour back."

A cold chill trickled through her veins like ice water as she straightened. "Did he say where he was going?"

"No. No, he didn't. Is something wrong, Emma?"

"Yes, I think I've made a big mistake."

Under the old straw hat, Fritz's ruined face creased with confusion, and concern.

"Oh, Fritz . . ." She shook her head miserably. "Why don't people appreciate what they have when they have it? How could I have been such a fool?"

"Is there something I can do?"

"Yeah, you can find Sam and bring him back, wherever he is," she said hopelessly, and turned to go.

Walking slowly back up the road, she hardly noticed the clear, sweet morning air, the chorus of birdsong in the green shade of the trees.

After all, how could she blame him? What man would want to be saddled with an emotional wreck? Even though she felt like a new woman today, she couldn't kid herself. She had a long way to go. And she couldn't expect Sam to do any more. But why did it have to take until now, when it was too late, for her to realize that she loved him?

The lake and sky dissolved into one as she wandered over to the old willow and leaned against the scarred gray trunk. But after a moment she fought back the tears and stood straight. What was wrong with her? Was she going to wimp out now, after making all this progress?

It was time to stop hiding away and go after what she wanted. And if that meant tracking him down all the way to L.A., she'd do it! On foot, if necessary.

She sniffed hard and wiped at her tears with the back of her hand, then jumped at the sound of a familiar irate voice behind her.

"Emma, tell this big galoot to put me down!"

"SAM!" SHE WHIRLED around to see Fritz striding over from the drive with Sam slung over his shoulder, fireman-fashion.

As she ran toward them Fritz dumped his captive onto his feet on the grass, but kept a tight hold on his collar with one massive fist.

Sam shot the other man an exasperated look as he tried to tug his shirt straight, before turning to her. "Emma, what's all this about? Your bodyguard here just hauled me out of my Jeep and carried me down the driveway. Will somebody tell me what's happening?"

She barely had time to register the confusion and annoyance on Sam's flushed face before she launched herself bodily into his arms and would have sent him reeling, but for Fritz's steadying grip.

Wrapping herself around him, she covered his face with kisses. "You didn't leave!"

He reared back a little, still looking stunned and confused, but his arms curved naturally around her to hold her close. "Of course, I didn't leave."

"Will that be all, Emma?"

She blinked and looked up into Fritz's amused eyes. "Oh Fritz, you found him for me. Thank you! Thank you so much."

He nodded, with a rare grin of satisfaction. "No problem. Let me know if there's anything else I can do." With that, he let go of Sam's collar.

Sam winced and began rotating his head. "Do you know anything about treating whiplash?"

But Fritz only chuckled at his dry tone and winked at him. "I have work to do. I'll see you later."

With a dazed look, Sam watched him walk away, then shook his head as if to clear it before turning back to her. "So what's this all about?"

She unwound her legs from his and put her feet back on the ground, but Sam still held her close and she tightened her arms around him, resting her head against his shoulder, in case he vanished again like a waking dream.

"I thought you'd gone. I thought you'd left."

She felt him shake his head slightly. "Without saying goodbye?" His voice deepened. "I'd never do something like that."

How could she have been so foolish? "I didn't know. I wasn't thinking, just panicking."

For a long moment there was silence and she looked up into the gravest expression she'd ever seen on his face.

"Would it matter so much to you if I did leave?"

Desperately she searched his eyes for some sign of what he felt, what he was thinking. "It would matter terribly."

"Why?" Once again that emotionless query. Something had subtly changed in him and it made her heart tighten with dread.

"Because I love you, Sam."

He took a deep breath, swallowed hard and closed his eyes, then very deliberately and gently put her away from him. "I think that you should give yourself some time. Time to really know how you feel."

He turned and began walking toward the willow, his hands in his pockets.

"I already know how I feel." A cold premonitory shudder raced through her. She ran a few steps to catch up.

He didn't look at her, just kept walking. "After everything you've been through, it wouldn't be fair of me to take advantage."

"But you're not!"

He wasn't listening. Everything was slipping away from her. There was only one way to convince him.

With a strength she didn't know she possessed, Emma grabbed his arm and turned him to face her. Before he had time to resist she pressed herself up against him, put her arms around his neck and kissed him, sliding her hot tongue along the line of his lips.

At first he held himself rigid, his hands at his sides, refusing to respond, but she'd learned a few tricks from him. She let her tongue linger at the corner of his mouth. "Come on, honey," she whispered, "open up for me."

She felt the quirk of his mouth in an unwilling smile, then with a sudden groan his restraint shattered. He opened his mouth to her, his arms came around her as if he wanted to absorb her into him, and her heart was filled to bursting. She kissed him slow and deep and fiercely.

After a little while she drew back a fraction, gasping for breath. "Does that answer your question?"

"Emma, are you sure? I don't want to push you," he murmured breathlessly against her mouth.

"I guess I'm going to have to prove it to you again."

But this time he didn't wait for her. He cupped his palm around her neck, pulled her urgently toward him and she lost herself in his arms, until nothing else existed around her. No a sound penetrated the little world filled by his heat, his scent and the taste of his mouth.

It could have been forever, or only a few seconds, as if this moment had always been and always would be; as if time stood still. She pressed closer, molding herself against him from head to toe, joining them together.

His strong, gentle hands were moving slowly over her, caressing her, as she pressed her palms against his back, gliding them possessively over the warm, smooth muscled flesh beneath his shirt, feeling herself awash in incredible sensations.

Need flowered deep inside and rushed into every part of her—a wonderful healing need that washed away the darkness and made her free and whole. She could feel the chains breaking, the bitter past receding at last and the future opening wide with bright promise.

In that slow, deep savoring she could finally open herself to the love pouring out of Sam in tangible waves, return that love freely with her mouth and her body, no longer afraid.

After a long time he slowly put her away from him, but not very far. His eyes were a keen brilliant blue in his tanned face, and filled with satisfaction. "We've got a lot to talk about—" that devilish grin broke through "—but I needed that to sustain me."

"I need a little more." She brushed her mouth across his, thrilled with the heady freedom to be teasing and provocative. "After all, I'm the one who has to do all the talking."

Easing apart a little, he took her hand and led her over to the willow. He straddled the branch, leaning back against the trunk to pull her up in front of him and settle her snugly between his thighs. She sank back against the warmth of his chest as he wrapped his arms around her from behind with a sigh of contentment.

The last wisps of morning mist had dissipated, the sun was well up in a clear blue sky and glinting off the sparkling surface of the water. The first houseboat could already be seen in the distance, heading out from the locks into the open lake.

"How do you feel?" he asked softly against her hair.

"A lot better, after my little temper tantrum last night. My room looks like it was hit by a bomb." She smiled a little ruefully, but without an ounce of regret. "I don't care. It was a small price to pay for finally unloading that burden."

"I'll help you clean up."

"Okay." She tipped her head up and gently traced his jaw with a fingertip. "But it might take all day," she said, softly and provocatively reveling in her newly discovered sensuality.

"I hope so." Then the smile disappeared from his face as he searched hers with grave concern. "I still can't believe there was no one to talk to."

She sighed and leaned her head back against him as she gazed out on the far horizon and hugged his arm closer. "I talked to you."

"I mean before."

"How could I? All our friends, everyone we knew thought we were the perfect couple, thought he was a great guy, the best of husbands." She drew in a deep breath of the sweet fresh morning air, feeling an unaccustomed lightness. For the first time she could talk about it, think about it, without every muscle tightening into a knot of anger. "I was always being told what a lucky woman I was. I thought so, too. I really believed we had the perfect marriage. I was happy."

"Were you writing during that time?"

She shook her head. "Life with Larry was one long round of travel and business entertaining. I didn't really have much time. In the beginning, when we were first married, I did some free-lance journalism. But soon it became obvious that there was no time even for that. It didn't matter to me at the time. I can hardly believe it now, but it didn't. I thought I was so lucky."

"Larry was the lucky one. He didn't deserve someone like you." His words were harsh and uncompromising.

"You're right. He didn't deserve someone like me. I just wish I could have felt this way before. Last year I ran into our old family doctor in town. He'd been retired for a couple of years. I hadn't seen him for a while and he allowed me to buy him a cup of coffee and catch up on gossip. Boy, did we ever." A jolt of bitterness went through her at the memory.

"What happened?"

"During the course of the conversation he let slip that Larry had had a vasectomy. Naturally he thought I knew." She took a deep breath and let it out on a sigh. "I didn't."

"Emma . . ."

"I know. You're thinking what kind of a blind fool I must have been."

"No, I'm not—"

"When I realized there was a problem I had myself tested and found out that *I* was fine. But Larry didn't want to put himself through the tests. I understood how hard it was on his pride. He said that we didn't need children, that we were happy. And with all the traveling that we did . . ." She shook her head and swallowed hard, but there were no tears left for that final, unforgivable betrayal. Just the lingering bitter regret for what might have been.

"How could you keep up the pretense of mourning him after that? That swine didn't deserve to have his good name protected." He shifted behind her and she could feel the tension in his body, his voice low with anger. "When I think of the hell he put you through . . ."

"How could I tell them what he'd done? How could I tell his mother that her beloved son, her beloved *dead* son, was a lying adulterer?"

"Considering how she treats you, no one would blame you if you did."

"No matter how I feel about her, I couldn't do that."

He sighed. "You're right, of course, but it still makes me angry."

"I know. It made me angry, too. But she wasn't the only one. How could I tell Fritz that he'd risked his life trying to save a liar and a cheat? That the man he'd served so faithfully for eight years, and revered as a friend, could have been so duplicitous? Besides, I blamed myself. I thought there had to be something wrong with me."

His arms tightened around her. "That's the part that makes me angriest of all. I hope you see things a little differently now."

"I do. Thanks to you."

"Me! What did I do?"

She smiled and rubbed her head against his chin. "Nothing much, except that from the moment we met, you badgered and bullied me into facing the truth and bringing it out into the open. If it hadn't been for you I'd still be cowering in my little retreat, fooling myself that I was doing just fine. You saved my life. Thank you."

"Don't thank me. I'm just the guy who fell in love with you." His voice was gruff with emotion as he tightened his arms possessively around her.

He made her feel so special, so safe. "You brought magic into my life, Sam. I could never forget that." She turned her head and kissed him softly, sweetly.

After a few moments he drew back and looked off into the distance with narrowed eyes.

He cleared his throat. "You know, Emma, when I went out this morning I drove around and . . . I had a lot of time to think."

"What were you thinking about?"

"About us, about you."

"And?"

He took a deep breath, but when he spoke his voice was carefully noncommittal. "I think you should take time to yourself to sort things out, to figure out what you want."

A cold warning shiver ran down her spine. They were back to that again. She thought she'd convinced him. But maybe he needed a break, too. Could she blame the man if he wanted her to sort herself out before coming to him?

She leaned her head on his shoulder and looked up at him. "Would you rather I did that?"

"It's not a question of what I want. It's a question of what you need, what you want." Nothing in his steady gaze gave his thoughts or feelings away.

For a moment the swirling clouds of guilt and confusion made her hesitate, and then she shifted upright and turned to face him squarely. For most of her adult life she'd put others' needs before her own, and suffered the consequences.

"No, it's not what I want. I want to be with you while I work on all those things. I don't want to be alone anymore."

"I'll be here for as long as you want me to be here."

"Well, then, that'll be forever." Her voice caught a little on the word.

"But if it's not, I'll understand."

Suddenly she felt sick and afraid. "Sam, what do you mean, what are you getting at? Don't you love me anymore? Has all this made you change your mind?"

"No! I love you even more. But *you* might change your mind. When you're feeling better about all this . . ."

She gasped and gave a weak little laugh. "You think this is just gratitude because you helped me get through a bad time?"

"It's possible. It's been known to happen." He swallowed hard, but kept his voice casual. He was trying to be strong for her and it frustrated her.

She shook her head vigorously. "That's not it."

"How do you know?"

For a moment she could only stare at him helplessly. Her happiness hung in the balance. How on earth could she convince him?

She took a deep breath. "I don't blame you for being skeptical. I spent a lot of time denying that I cared about you. But I realize now that you were right. I could never have given myself like that, had I not loved you."

"What makes you so sure now?" he asked, his voice quietly, deadly serious.

She turned more completely around on her perch and clutched his shoulders, willing him to understand. "Because that's not me. You were right about that, too." She gave him a rueful smile. "I was just too afraid to face up to it. But you see, for a long time I didn't know who I was. At first I thought that any desire for a sexual relationship was completely dead in me. But then you came and everything changed, from the very first moment."

"The very first?" He raised a skeptical eyebrow and smiled.

"Yes. Even in that damn pit my body responded to you. You touched me, and I burned. And I thought . . . I thought that meant I'd somehow become corrupted by what Larry had done, by the way I found out. And then when you started probing into Belial I found myself thinking for the first time that the story hadn't simply burst from my imagination. But that it was connected with what I'd become, a person filled with a deep propensity for evil and hate." A shudder ran through her. "A warped . . . monster."

"Oh, Emma . . ."

"I told myself that all I felt for you was lust. I was too afraid to believe that I was beginning to care about you and enjoy being with you. I fought hard against those feelings because I didn't ever want to believe in love again. I'd been in love before, and I thought I was loved in return, but that was a sham. A farce."

"You can't get over that kind of betrayal in one night."

A wave of hopelessness swept over her as she stared into his somber blue eyes that were silently watching her. She wasn't convincing him, and right now her whole life depended on coming up with the right words. She gripped his shoulders tighter, her body taut with desperation.

"But don't you see? Now I *know* that I could never have come to you and made love with you like that, feeling the way I did, if I weren't in love with you. I was afraid to believe before, but I'm not afraid anymore." Her voice strengthened with conviction. "And I can't and will not lose you."

For a moment he fixed her with a still, steady look and she hardly dared to breathe, for fear of what he might be thinking, what he might say.

Suddenly he swung off the branch and pulled her off with him, cradling her in his arms. Automatically, she wrapped her arms around his neck as he began to walk, carrying her with him. She could feel the tension in his body and the excitement bubbling inside her, the tremulous hope.

She hugged him tight and murmured in his ear. "Where are we going?"

"Where we can be private. Where else?"

He carried her into the cabin and upstairs to the loft bedroom, then sank onto the futon and slowly lowered her to the mattress.

"Does this mean that you finally believe me, you stubborn man?"

Kneeling above her, his hands on either side, he stared into her eyes, examining, searching for something deep down. Then his mouth curved in that crooked smile that made her heart melt with love for him.

"I hope you're sure about this, because once I have you, I'll never let you go."

She cupped his face in her hands, pouring every ounce of sincerity she possessed into the words. "I'm very sure, and I love you very much." And then, because she needed to know, she asked. "Sam, about Robyn . . . It's only been a little over a year. . . . Are *you* sure?"

He put a gentle finger to her lips. "It's because of Robyn that I know what love is all about. She taught me how to give love and now I want to give it to you." Tears sprang into her eyes as he continued. "And Robyn—" he smiled "—I know she's up there rooting for us."

"I hope she knows that I love you, and I plan to take very good care of you."

"Let's just take very good care of each other, okay? Starting now . . ."

"I won't argue with that."

"Can you do that—not argue?"

He grinned and she pulled him down to her.

"Oh, shut up." She sighed blissfully against his lips, giving herself over to heaven.

Epilogue

REACHING THE CREST of the quarry hill, Sam veered off the track onto the path he knew so well now, picking his way carefully through the deep snow with his heavy boots.

In the gathering dusk, as he penetrated farther into the thicket of bare trees and skeletal sumachs, he suddenly became aware that it was very quiet in here this evening. Not a breath of breeze in the frigid air, not a single birdcall on this gloomy January evening.

He stopped and listened. Nothing. A sudden feeling of foreboding curled up his spine. Too quiet. *Knock it off, you jackass.* But he quickened his pace as he made for the tip of the hill. He could see the cedar grove now—and she wasn't there.

"Emma?" His voice was swallowed up by the empty air as he swiveled around, carefully searching the bush around him. Nothing, just him and the waiting silence. "Emma!"

Everything was so still. Where was she?

A frisson of alarm made him uneasy, but he took a deep breath and turned back, smiling grimly at how quickly he could be brought to the brink of panic. She'd gone somewhere else, maybe into town. He shoved his gloved hands into his jacket pockets and began to retrace his footsteps in the knee-deep snow.

It was getting dark, she was probably at home already. He quickened his pace at thoughts of Emma waiting there for him. He was one lucky guy, no doubt about it.

With a sharp crack, a twig snapped to his right, shattering the silence. He stopped and peered through the growing dark toward the huge round hollow ringed by towering spruce and dark cedars, to find only snow and blue shadows, and an even deeper stillness.

It really was quiet in here tonight. He pulled his collar closer, suddenly feeling chilled, and began walking again. Emma was waiting for him at home . . . home where it was warm, safe. There was something about this place tonight that gave him the creeps, but he tried to subdue the unease.

Suddenly the silence was shattered by a roar, and a figure hurtled toward him out of a clump of cedars. He yelled as his heart shot into his throat, his feet cleared the ground and he landed sprawled on his backside in the snow.

"Got you, you rat." Emma's laughing voice came to him through the pounding of his heart. He looked up to see her standing above him with her feet apart and her arms crossed, grinning from ear to ear.

"For what?" he gasped.

"For the shower this morning."

"You asked for that." He squinted up at her with a lazy smile. "Just like you asked for this."

Before she knew it he surged to his feet, moving like lightning as his hand shot out to grab her. She squealed and swiveled out of the way.

"You filthy sneak," she gasped. Laughing, she ran from him, putting the trunk of a sturdy maple between them.

His breath came in little pants as he stood poised and smiling. "You can't escape me, Emma." His smile was demonic, his voice slipping into the velvety roughness of Belial. "I am going to get you and then . . ."

"And then what?" She taunted him from the other side of the tree. Slowly, deliberately, she darted out her tongue and ran it over her upper lip with a wicked smile. She was suddenly flooded with warmth. Would she ever get enough of this man? Her smile broadened and a ping of pure happiness shot through her. Never.

He sprang like a striking cobra, caught her and hauled her up against the rough bark of the tree, trapping her with his body. "And then this."

His mouth came down on hers in a long slow kiss that melted the snow around them. A kiss just as passionate and lascivious as his threat had promised. In her whole life she'd never known she was capable of such depth of feeling. Impossible to find the words that would describe how much she loved him. In the face of such a profound emotion she felt very small. Finally he lifted his mouth from hers.

"You brute," she murmured against his lips, and felt him smile.

"If you're through abusing me, I have some news."

"What is it?" She nuzzled the side of his jaw, rough with beard shadow.

His small sigh whispered across her face. "*Belial's* been nominated for an Oscar."

She stopped nuzzling and slowly raised her head to look at him. Only a tiny smile curved his mouth, but his eyes shone bright blue with pent-up excitement.

"Sam...that's wonderful." His smile broadened. She shook her head, feeling a little bemused. Then she laughed and kissed him hard on the lips before pulling away, breathless. "That's wonderful. Darling, I'm so proud of you."

"You were nominated, too."

"What!"

He nodded. "For the screenplay."

"I don't believe it." She shook her head. This was incredible.

"It's true. Best adaptation. We did it, honey."

"Are you sure?"

"Come home and read the fax yourself." He grinned while she could only stare in disbelief for a full minute.

Then she spun away from him and jumped up, punching the air. "Yes!"

Laughing with delight, she rushed him again, throwing her arms around him and sending him staggering off-balance.

Sam chuckled. "Hey, take it easy, you crazy woman."

"Tell me I'm not dreaming."

But she didn't give him a chance to answer as she drew him down to her, and he didn't need much urging, but squeezed her close and ravished her lips.

Through the layers of clothing between them she could feel him getting hard, feel the wet heat between her thighs. She moaned into his mouth and wrapped a leg around him, straining to get closer.

"Here?" Sam's ragged whisper brushed her face. "You're crazy." And yet he molded her buttocks in his hands, pressing her closer.

"Why not? No one will come." Her voice came out in small gasps as she swiveled her hips against him.

"You'll freeze." He pulled off his gloves, tugged down the zipper of her parka and slipped one shaking hand under her sweater to curve hotly around her bare breast.

A little sound of pleasure escaped her throat. "I'm depending on you to keep me warm."

"I have to do everything around here."

"Stop complaining. I let you move into the big house, didn't I?" She reached down to unfasten his fly and quickly, unerringly, took his rigid flesh in her hand.

He gave a small chuckle and then a long, shuddering sigh as his eyes closed in ecstasy.

EMMA LOOKED THROUGH the rear window of the limo at the receding crowd of fans and paparazzi outside the Dorothy Chandler Pavilion, then turned back to snuggle into Sam's embrace.

Fritz took up most of the opposite seat, massively resplendent in black tie, and beside him sat four golden statuettes. She could hardly believe that one of them was hers.

"I still think you should have won for Best Actor." She kicked off her heels and rested her stocking feet on Sam's outstretched legs.

"I agree. What has Mel Gibson got that you haven't?"

Emma had to smile at Fritz's indignation. He was as ferociously loyal to Sam now as he'd ever been to her.

"Right now he's got the Best Actor Oscar," Sam said dryly.

"So what?" She leaned her cheek against the fine black wool of his tuxedo jacket. "You've got Best Director and Best Picture, what more could you want?"

"How about a baby?"

His soft words made her look up to see him watching her with a glowing, possessive smile, and her heart expanded. The past two years had been...incredible. Through the pain and the tears and the healing, and most of all through the happiness, Sam had been there. Solid and real, always loving, always there. The Oscar was really nice, but the prize she cherished most was Sam's love.

Wrapping her arms around him, she cuddled even closer. "I think that can be arranged."

Fritz sank back into the plush seat with a big sigh of satisfaction, looking from her to Sam with a benign smile.

Sam's arms tightened around her and his lips brushed her temple with a contented murmur: "Then I have everything I could ever want."

"Everything except the rights to my new book," Emma taunted with a sly grin.

"Don't remind me. I'm still negotiating with that agent of yours." He gave a dry chuckle. "And this time, *she* gets the pit."

HARLEQUIN®

Temptation®

Secret Fantasies

Do you have a secret fantasy?

Reporter Darien Hughes does. While celebrating her thirtieth birthday, she spots a gorgeous man across the crowded restaurant. For fun, she writes about this "secret fantasy man" in her column. But Darien gets a shock when "Sam" shows up at the paper! Enjoy #530 NIGHT GAMES by Janice Kaiser, available in March 1995.

Everybody has a secret fantasy. And you'll find them all in Temptation's exciting new yearlong miniseries, Secret Fantasies. Beginning January 1995, one book each month focuses on the hero or heroine's innermost romantic fantasies....

Take 4 bestselling love stories FREE

Plus get a FREE surprise gift!

Special Limited-time Offer

Mail to Harlequin Reader Service®

3010 Walden Avenue
P.O. Box 1867
Buffalo, N.Y. 14269-1867

YES! Please send me 4 free Harlequin Temptation® novels and my free surprise gift. Then send me 4 brand-new novels every month, which I will receive before they appear in bookstores. Bill me at the low price of $2.44 each plus 25¢ delivery and applicable sales tax, if any.* That's the complete price and a savings of over 10% off the cover prices—quite a bargain! I understand that accepting the books and gift places me under no obligation ever to buy any books. I can always return a shipment and cancel at any time. Even if I never buy another book from Harlequin, the 4 free books and the surprise gift are mine to keep forever.

142 BPA AJHR

Name	(PLEASE PRINT)	
Address	Apt. No.	
City	State	Zip

MOVE OVER, MELROSE PLACE!

> Apartment for rent
> One bedroom
> Bachelor Arms
> 555-1234

Come live and love in L.A. with the tenants of Bachelor Arms.
Enjoy a year's worth of wonderful love stories and meet
colorful neighbors you'll bump into again and again.

First, we'll introduce you to Bachelor Arms residents Josh,
Tru and Garrett—three to-die-for and determined bachelor
buddies—who do everything they can to avoid walking down
the aisle. Bestselling author
Kate Hoffmann brings us these romantic comedies in the
new continuity series from Temptation:

THE STRONG SILENT TYPE #529 (March 1995)

A HAPPILY UNMARRIED MAN #533 (April 1995)

Soon to move into Bachelor Arms are the heroes and
heroines in books by our most popular authors—
JoAnn Ross, Candace Schuler and Judith Arnold. You'll
read a new book every month.

Don't miss the goings-on at Bachelor Arms.

If you've missed Harlequin Temptation's first Bachelor Arms book, here is your
chance to order #525 *Bachelor Husband* by Kate Hoffmann. Please send your name,
address, zip or postal code along with a check or money order (please do not send
cash) for $3.25 for each book ordered ($3.75 in Canada), plus 75¢ postage and
handling ($1.00 in Canada), payable to Harlequin Books, to:

In the U.S.:	In Canada:
3010 Walden Avenue	P. O. Box 613
P. O. Box 9047	Fort Erie, Ontario
Buffalo, NY 14269-9047	L2A 5X3

Please specify book title with your order.
Canadian residents add applicable federal and provincial taxes.

HARLEQUIN®
Temptation

BA-2

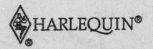

Harlequin invites you to the most
romantic wedding of the season.

Rope the cowboy of your dreams in
Marry Me, Cowboy!

A collection of 4 brand-new stories,
celebrating weddings, written by:

New York Times bestselling author

JANET DAILEY

and favorite authors

Margaret Way
Anne McAllister
Susan Fox

Be sure not to miss Marry Me, Cowboy!
coming this April

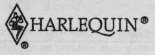

Fifty red-blooded, white-hot, true-blue hunks
from every State in the Union!

Look for MEN MADE IN AMERICA! Written by some
of our most popular authors, these stories feature some
of the strongest, sexiest men, each from a different state
in the union!

Two titles available every month at your favorite
retail outlet.

In February, look for:

THE SECURITY MAN by Dixie Browning
(North Carolina)
A CLASS ACT by Kathleen Eagle (North Dakota)

In March, look for:

TOO NEAR THE FIRE by Lindsay McKenna (Ohio)
A TIME AND A SEASON by Curtiss Ann Matlock
(Oklahoma)

You won't be able to resist MEN MADE IN AMERICA!

Bestselling Author

JoAnn Ross

Delivers a story so exciting, so thrilling, it'll have you begging for more....

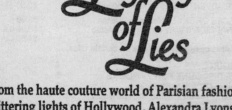

Legacy of Lies

From the haute couture world of Parisian fashion to the glittering lights of Hollywood, Alexandra Lyons will find fame, fortune and love. But desire and scandal will shatter her life unless she can uncover her legacy of lies.

Look for it at your favorite retail outlet this February.

HARLEQUIN®

Don't miss these Harlequin favorites by some of our most distinguished authors!
And now, you can receive a discount by ordering two or more titles!

HT#25577	WILD LIKE THE WIND by Janice Kaiser	$2.99	☐
HT#25589	THE RETURN OF CAINE O'HALLORAN by JoAnn Ross	$2.99	☐
HP#11626	THE SEDUCTION STAKES by Lindsay Armstrong	$2.99	☐
HP#11647	GIVE A MAN A BAD NAME by Roberta Leigh	$2.99	☐
HR#03293	THE MAN WHO CAME FOR CHRISTMAS by Bethany Campbell	$2.89	☐
HR#03308	RELATIVE VALUES by Jessica Steele	$2.89	☐
SR#70589	CANDY KISSES by Muriel Jensen	$3.50	☐
SR#70598	WEDDING INVITATION by Marisa Carroll	$3.50 U.S. $3.99 CAN.	☐
HI#22230	CACHE POOR by Margaret St. George	$2.99	☐
HAR#16515	NO ROOM AT THE INN by Linda Randall Wisdom	$3.50	☐
HAR#16520	THE ADVENTURESS by M.J. Rodgers	$3.50	☐
HS#28795	PIECES OF SKY by Marianne Willman	$3.99	☐
HS#28824	A WARRIOR'S WAY by Margaret Moore	$3.99 U.S. $4.50 CAN.	☐

(limited quantities available on certain titles)

	AMOUNT	$
DEDUCT:	10% DISCOUNT FOR 2+ BOOKS	$
ADD:	POSTAGE & HANDLING	$
	($1.00 for one book, 50¢ for each additional)	
	APPLICABLE TAXES*	$_____
	TOTAL PAYABLE	$_____
	(check or money order—please do not send cash)	

To order, complete this form and send it, along with a check or money order for the total above, payable to Harlequin Books, to: **In the U.S.:** 3010 Walden Avenue, P.O. Box 9047, Buffalo, NY 14269-9047; **In Canada:** P.O. Box 613, Fort Erie, Ontario, L2A 5X3.

Name: _____

Address: _____ City: _____

State/Prov.: _____ Zip/Postal Code: _____

*New York residents remit applicable sales taxes.
 Canadian residents remit applicable GST and provincial taxes.

HBACK-JM2